Close of Play

PJ Whiteley

First published in Great Britain in 2015
by Urbane Publications Ltd
Suite 3, Brown Europe House,
33/34 Gleamingwood Drive,
Chatham, Kent ME5 8RZ

This book is a work of fiction. Names, characters, places, organisations and incidents either are products of the author's imagination or are used fictitiously. Apart from historical fact, any resemblance to actual events, organisations, or persons living or dead, is entirely coincidental

A CIP catalogue record for this book is available
from the British Library.

Paperback ISBN 978-1-909273-52-8
mobi ISBN 978-1-909273-54-2
epub ISBN 978-1-909273-53-5

Design and Typeset by Chandler Book Design
Cover design by Chandler Book Design

FSC

leading
e from
forest-
sations,

To Michael.

In our thoughts every day.

CONTENTS

Acknowledgements

First of all, I'd like to thank Rose. It's extremely unlikely I'd have been able to complete a romantic comedy without being married to a relationship therapist with a wicked sense of humour. As it turned out, watching quality TV drama with the aid of your comments was how I learned to do dialogue.

Then I have to thank Mum and the rest of my large family for encouraging me to read more than just the sports pages as a boy – though will she finally accept that I actually did so; a lot more than she thinks I did? I guess that's one family myth that will persist. I still maintain that Jennings books are better than Just William. That controversy also continues.

I would also like to thank some of the brilliant writers who've inspired me, in the approximate order in which I encountered them: Anthony Buckeridge, Willard Price, Dick Clement & Ian Le Frenais, Bob Dylan, John Steinbeck, David Nobbs, George Orwell, David Lodge, Norman Lewis, Iris Murdoch, Charlotte Brontë, Simone de Beauvoir,

Charles Dickens, Isabel Allende, Mario Vargas Llosa, Gabriel García Márquez, Manuel Puig, Donna Tartt, Miguel de Cervantes, John Walsh, Javier Marías – and of course the master of comedy himself Albert Camus. Many more would deserve mention, but these are the writers who produced works that moved me, or caused me to think differently, or made my jaw drop with astonishment, or caused me to laugh out loud, or in the case of La Peste, all four. And yes, that book was a recommendation from Mum. It is obviously a puzzle that the French intelligentsia never took to cricket, the most complete existentialist metaphor. If they had, perhaps Europe's problems would be a touch lighter than they currently are. There's a book to be written there, but by someone cleverer than me.

Many thanks to the Ampthill writers, whose encouragement and inspiration helped me finish an opus first begun in 1998. I didn't set out to write a historical novel – it just took me a long time to complete. Helping me over the finishing line were (and I hope I don't omit an important name): Rachel Lewis, Simon Michael, Emma Marriott, Emma Riddell, Alanna Collen (great advice on key moments in the book, thank you!), Katie Packman, Jo Walker, the Helens Armitage, Wetherill and Manley, Tess Crosbie, Manou Chambon, Jeremy Ramsden, Samantha and Norbert Oetting and the many people who've attended our Beer and Books events.

I would like to thank Bob Daws for encouragement and the commendation for the cover. A curious detail to the genesis of Close of Play is that it was originally conceived, shortly after the screening of the two series of Outside Edge, with the idea of Bob as the one to play the title role. By coincidence I came to know him 15 years later through the Ampthill Literary Festival.

Thanks to the irrepressible Sarah Mackinlay-Crouch for feedback and encouragement after reading a draft, and for her friendship and sense of humour. There's a free box set of Genesis albums for you!

Thanks to Judy Foster for checking the sections on social work & adoption; and to Steven Sylvester for appraising the parts on fast bowling.

Thanks to all the unsung people who run cricket clubs throughout the country. Specifically some of those who were great teammates: the Kingstons and Williams at Gravesend in the 1970s, those at Dimanchian CC, Gary at Hogarth (surname sadly forgotten), Julian Guiste et al at Sisserou in Dagenham, Richard Bowers and the Overingtons and others at Oakwoodhill, the guys from Streatham Cricket Club, and everyone at Ampthill Town Cricket Club.

Finally, of course, a massive thanks to Matthew Smith for giving me this opportunity; for his wise advice on plot development, and to all associates at Urbane Publications.

PJ Whiteley

'If you make a mistake in the corridor of uncertainty, you may end up on the highway of regret.'

(with sincere apologies to
Geoff Boycott and Bob Dylan)

Preface

EVERYTHING ABOUT MY appearance, to the smallest detail, declares 'Old school'. Short hair, side-parting. Tweed or corduroy jackets with leather elbow patches. Crease in the trousers, even at weekends. A shirt with a collar, and usually with a tie, which may sport a crest or badge associated with a club, school, or ex-alumni association.

You will form an opinion about me before my speaking a word, but some of these are likely to be mistaken. I don't resist technology, unless it is hideous; I don't dislike young people (quite the contrary), and I don't hate change. I do, however, dislike vulgarity. Matters far beyond my control have determined that, in the late 20th and early 21st Century, British society features an apparently unstoppable rise in vulgarity: punk rock, celebrities, tabloid newspapers, the National Lottery, soap operas. Tabloid newspapers writing about celebrities, the Lottery and soap operas. Militant atheists who decide they are cleverer than God. BBC executives who pander to the clamour for more vulgarity for fear of appearing old-fashioned.

I believe in good manners, an appreciation of literature, a concern for society and the divinity of Jesus Christ. Not because these matters are old-fashioned, but because they are good. I was born to be on a collision course with the times I grew up in, but not all the jolts and de-railings have been unpleasant, as you'll begin to see as we pick up the story, around 20 years ago.

I

Walk, don't walk

I could hear the dressing room banter from the lads, before I entered the pavilion for the season's penultimate game.

'Do you think she'd go out with me, if I asked?'

'You'd have more chance if you didn't ask.'

'No but seriously?'

'Yes, but seriously – no. You're not in her league.'

'Leagues? There are leagues?'

''fraid so, son.'

'So, if there are leagues, is there promotion-relegation? Am I at least in with a chance of making the play-offs?'

'Yea, but she's Premiership, and you're Vauxhall Conference.'

'More like Mid-Sussex League Division 3,' chipped in another voice.

I could hear laughter. Then someone saying: "Ere, where's Col? Not like him to be late. He'd better turn up soon or Bodger will have to open and he is a) still pissed from last night; and b) not here yet either.'

I appeared on the threshold. 'Ah, 'ere 'e is,' my team mate

Tony announced as I appeared. 'Sight for sore eyes. We're batting.'

I started to change and strap on the pads.

Derek Cooper, the skipper, enquired: 'Have we got a full team yet?'

There were sniggers around the small room, with its waft of aftershave, beer, canvas and leather. 'We got ten, Del. I think that's as far as we'll get today,' said Greg. 'Might have to call someone up from the seconds. It's only a friendly.'

'Isn't Bodger playing?' he demanded.

There were hoots of laughter. 'I tell ya,' said Greg. 'If Bodger's alive after last night, medical science ought to know. State he was in. Jeez!'

'Thought that German barmaid was going to have 'im barred,' offered Tony.

'Yea, she was scary.'

'Oh, I dunno. Thought she was cute.'

'Get away!'

'Well she can have me, any time.'

'Not saying much. You'd have anyone!'

'Fair point,' said Tony, good naturedly. At this point Eric Gray, he who was known as Bodger, appeared, looking grey, ill and triumphant. There were more hoots as he slumped on a chair near the door, lit a cigarette and supported his chin with his hands. 'Don't tell me we're fielding,' he said.

'No, we're not,' said Derek.

'Thank Christ for that. I'll just go have a kip.'

'Yea well, you can't. You're number three.'

'What?' he looked up, aghast.

'You're so easy to wind up you are.'

'Bastard.'

'Also you're fined. Three times over.'

'What for?'

'Turning up late, swearing at the captain, being in an offensive state.'

'Great start to the afternoon.'

'Yea, well. I'm the captain. I'm not nice underneath, you know.'

'Never imagined you were, Del-Boy.'

'Be fair Derek,' said Tony. 'He's always in an offensive state. You can't fine 'im for that.'

'Shut up and get your pads on.'

The team had a comprehensive system of fines: for turning up late, dropping a catch, being rude to the captain, being too deferent to the captain ('arse-licking'), running the captain out, running the best batsman out, not chasing hard in the field, and generally for other incidents in the course of a match that prompted the captain, the on-field Fines Master, to decide that he didn't like the cut of your jib. There was also a fine for not buying a jug when you were due. Given that the cost of eight pints of beer was considerably greater than the standard fine – 30 pence – it was often observed that the incentive arrangement needed adjustment; but generally it was concluded that the public shame should serve as incentive enough. These arrangements held for match day. For the tour, where 14 or so players were sharing accommodation for four or five days, an entirely new range of opportunities for levying imposts sprang into being. Many offences were delightfully contradictory: going to bed too early, staying up all night; dressing too slovenly at breakfast, dressing too smart. Others included phoning home too much and partaking of alcoholic beverages in the course of a game (this rule tended to be relaxed towards the end of the tour). These were the typical crimes, but the Fines Master, a duty which on tour was rotated on a 24-hour basis, was allowed considerable discretion to invent arbitrary misdemeanours, such as a garish logo on your cricket boots, swearing in a foreign language (I once uttered the expletive '*merde*' when dropping a catch) or 'looking at me in a funny way'. In a typical year, fines yielded more revenue than the annual subscriptions, helping to pay for the new pitch and modernised pavilion.

I walked out with Tony to the middle and took my guard, scratching the damp earth and breaking the fresh white painted line of the popping crease. It was well into September, and the air was chilly. The rain had relented but the wind had not. Yellow and brown leaves studded the green outfield and the spikes of my boots sank gratefully into the mud.

I love to open the batting, as I dislike waiting my turn. Normally, I felt relaxed as the bowler began his run-up, but on this occasion I felt unprepared, struggling to focus with my eyes and adjusting to the light, even though it was not so bright. It was unlike me to be late to the ground. I made a vague link in my mind between my lack of organisation and sporadic feelings of melancholy in recent weeks and days, occasionally strong, especially in the evenings. I tried hard to concentrate on the familiar task of focusing on the small red object being hurled towards me, inwardly repeating the more effective mantras. 'See it early, hit it late,' Geoffrey Boycott had said. Still the best advice.

The bowler turned out to be one of those irritating exponents incapable of real speed or guile but who, on this day, hoped the wind would play tricks for him. He overpitched the first ball and I drove solidly, straight at the fielder. The next ball was a repeat but I found the gap and the ball fizzed quickly over the wet grass to find the boundary. The next seemed identical and I drove more ambitiously. There was a click and a thud and a shout as the wicket keeper took the catch.

I did not turn round to see the joyous fielders. For the first time in my life I waited for the decision. The umpire pointed his finger towards me. 'I find you guilty of driving over-confidently, treating the bowler without respect, being an inadequate and lonely person; and, moreover, of being out,' the raised digit seemed to say. I trudged back to the pavilion.

'Short and sweet,' commented Derek, as I arrived in the pavilion.

'It was short, anyway,' I replied, grumpily, falling into a morose silence.

When our turn came to field I stood cold and unhappy, throwing the ball in anger when it came to me. I was displeased with myself; not walking when out was unchristian and against the amateur code; I should have been better company for my colleagues and less grumpy in the field. They didn't particularly notice, however; each absorbed in his own personal battle as a bowler, or just trying to keep warm in the field. The game drifted to a draw. Just one left of the season.

I showered at the pavilion, changed and returned home, not stopping for a drink in the club bar, keen to be home and with my own company. As soon as I was, however, sat in my armchair, pretending to concentrate on a news report about the terrible events in the former Yugoslavia, I felt lonely; and of course, guilty that I could not feel happier about my lot compared with those living in daily fear of warlords and their armies.

I met Graham in the pub later, as I often did on a Saturday, for a beer, a chat and a game of chess. It was the one evening that he typically did not spend with his family, being in the routine of taking turns with his wife Jane, who would spend Sunday afternoons with her sister while Graham looked after the children. He was one of those eager, bearded chaps who is never tired, never depressed, never out of sorts. This was all the more remarkable given that he was wheelchair-bound, and had been since childhood. He was most extraordinarily resourceful and inventive, and quite the most intelligent person I had ever known. His home was a temple to gadgetry, many of the innovations designed by himself, with automatic doors, robot-controlled devices and the like. He was also an accomplished pianist and generous with his talent – sometimes helping at the church when our regular organist was ill. Given that he was a committed atheist, who preferred jazz, this was very decent of him indeed.

One of his most striking characteristics was a consistent ability to know of some new scheme or technology or whatever, which he would describe in great detail and would judge very firmly as either a remarkable innovation or an outright scam. His day job was in information technology of some kind, and he was often in demand by some consultancy or government. We took different views on automation. His attitude was: Technology can transform our quality of life. Mine was: We don't even make good use of humans, yet. We would debate the issue earnestly as young men but I guess, in retrospect, we were both right.

As I met him that evening he told me of some problem he had been having with a supplier, as a customer. I did not attend well, knowing that my duty mostly was to be quiet and not to comment and that, if I was needed in a professional capacity to support a claim, he would contact me with the details during working hours. He would often have a grievance over poor service from a company; not because he was eager to complain or seek compensation, but more typically because, being far more intelligent than the average corporate manager responsible for arranging customer services, he had thought of a far smarter way of organising things, and was quite genuinely baffled that it had not appeared obvious to anyone else.

He then offered some detail, as though I had pressed him for it, of technological developments in the banking industry. 'Before long,' he informed me. 'All our savings, mortgage accounts and bank accounts will be linked together and be available on the Internet. I won't have to visit the bank anymore! Just click on the screen at home. Brilliant for cripples like me.'

He pushed the bridge of his glasses firmly up his nose with his pudgy forefinger, its pink end whitening with the brief impact. Needless to say, I was not on the Internet, declining to take part in the craze for 'surfing' the so-called 'web', though I made a mental note to learn a little more about it.

'Shall I be black?' he asked.

'No,' I said firmly, straightening the chess board on the small wobbly table that sat between us. 'You will build your impenetrable Sicilian defence and we should be here 'til midnight. I'll be black.'

He won, as he customarily did. For all my supposedly cerebral air I have always been much better at sport than chess or crosswords; a fact that often surprises people but which I actually find rather pleasing. I took pleasure in confounding expectations.

There had been more of us in the late '60s and early '70s than you might think; we 'old school' chaps, though we were a minority at university: playing chess, attending debating societies, going to the opera, while the others organized sit-ins and went to Rolling Stones concerts. They revelled in their rock and roll, but never thought to attend the Royal Albert Hall to hear Jacqueline du Pré, missing perhaps the finest musical genius of their generation. They thought they were radical but I considered them childish. Anything – literally anything – would prompt a walk-out. They would protest over library opening hours as if it were a human rights issue. Although I do recall one heavily bearded, long-haired chap, in tee-shirt and jeans, confide in me that he voted Conservative at the 1970 election, when Ted Heath won. They were bewildering times.

For all Graham's intelligence, I sometimes wondered if he had a capacity for reflection, and whether he masked his emotion, or felt less, or dealt with it more effectively. I showed little myself, but that was reserve. I had been particularly keen to have company that evening, and had envisaged during the cold two hours spent in the field that I might dare to confess to him my increasing sense of desolation, especially in the gloomy evenings at home on my own, and request solace or advice. I wondered if the subject would have been as alien to him as the suggestion that we might skip the pub in search of a Turkish bath. Chaps don't talk about feelings; at least, not innermost feelings – only those that don't matter.

Could I make an exception, on this evening? There could not be a better friend. I could essay an oblique way in, perhaps. I offered: 'I'm not impatient to look at my personal finances, to be honest, whether it's on the internet or not. Makes you think about the future. And the thing about the future is ...'

'... that it's inherently unknowable,' said Graham, interrupting. 'Past trends are often a poor guide to what will happen, but as humans we're wired to rely on them.'

I felt he was missing my intended point, but to be fair I had not really articulated it. 'Yes but I mean,' I began. Could I really say 'What's the point of it all?' It would probably trigger an analysis of the asymmetric nature of market patterns. 'I've thought of selling the house,' I said instead.

'Good time to sell,' he said straight away. 'House prices are back above three times average earnings. Yours would fetch a packet.'

'Yes,' I said, becoming rather despairing.

'Can I say something Brian?' he asked suddenly, leaning forward towards me and brushing his brown, rounded beard with thumb and forefinger. 'It might not be a bad idea to move on, and I don't just mean because the price would be good. I mean, it's your Aunt Kath's old house, isn't it?'

'And her parents' before her.'

'Quite. Well, are you sure you want to be surrounded by the memories? Does it actually make it easier to live on your own?'

'I, er, haven't quite looked at it that way,' I said, somewhat taken aback. 'It's always seemed kind of blasphemous to sell, but it's hardly the place for an ageing bachelor.'

'I've lived on my own as well, Brian,' he said, stroking his beard quite vigorously. 'It can be better if it's somewhere that actually is your own.'

I stayed silent a little while, looking down into my drink, in equal part astounded at this new dimension to my companion and stung by the apposite nature of his remarks. A roar of conversation from the public bar erupted as a couple pushed open the door behind Graham and entered. The noise subsided as the door swung back.

'I'm sorry if I'm appearing to intrude,' he continued.

'No, not at all. I raised the subject myself after all. Good advice anyway. Can I buy you a drink?' I asked.

My worst fear materialised that night. I awoke before dawn and felt the depression anew. There was a softened quality to it, however; like the difference between drizzle and rain. I felt more comfortable and almost inured. My room was the back room, which was sizeable enough. I had left the master bedroom, with its grand bay window, empty since Aunt Kath had passed away, save for a few shelves of books and a rocking chair. I went to sit in it and listened for ghosts. I had no gift for the supernatural, and could see nothing but the dusty darkness, the frame of the window, the patterned wallpaper. I tried to hear her voice, but I could hear only the rattle of a milk cart.

She had a tendency to be indulgent towards me, but the exception was on grammatical points. I recalled one winter's afternoon, bursting into that same room after I had come in breathless from playing on the ice with some friends. 'We went up Sissons Hill and skated down the bank, Aunty Kath,' I gasped. 'And the pond at the bottom is frozen solid. Not bad for Sussex standards.'

She looked at me and frowned, placing hands on hips, and I awaited a lecture on the folly of our recklessness. Instead she said: 'Don't use a noun as an adjective dear, most especially a proper noun. It's most vulgar. Now go wash your hands while I make the tea.'

I enjoyed the memory. She had had a good innings, I thought. There would not have been rousing cheers on her walk to the pavilion, but the knowing observers would have given her a good hand. 'We never know when we will go,' she would often say. The certainty of our end is our very frame; but the emptiness of my stretched canvas filled me anew with despair. The sun re-emerged. I felt warm in my pyjamas and dressing gown and eventually dozed.

2

This is Elizabeth Giles

Tired and disconcerted, a feeling akin to jet lag, in the morning I went to church. Perhaps the spirit might revive the body, if he could be awakened by the 9.30 sung communion at All Saints. The Reverend Godfrey Charlton was an earnest and intelligent soul, younger than such a Christian name might indicate, and deserving of more attention than I gave. He would speak articulately and quickly, somewhat self-conscious of his learning; forever justifying his carefully couched assertions or questioning his authority to make them. It made him engaging as an individual but less than effective as a preacher. Some of my fellow congregation muttered at such indecisiveness since he had joined us in the spring, but I found such cautious phrasing and conscientiousness reassuring. Life is complex and I rather imagine that God is too.

'Christ said, "Judge not; and you shall not be judged",' Godfrey told us. 'This does not mean that one should never judge. We judge all the time; sometimes a little harshly -

I know I do myself. He was reminding us - and this is a personal reflection; you may wish to make your own - that the standards we set will often be the ones by which we are judged. Christ was not, I think, always meek and humble, but neither did he send curses upon humans for being weak. Indeed he was as complex as he was divine, and defies all attempts to paint him into a corner, and pretend he was a simple caricature.' This was a typical excerpt: wise but not necessarily inspirational.

He greeted me after the service. 'Hello Colin,' he called out warmly as he shook my hand outside the church door. I wondered if I could ever inform him that my name is not Colin.

'Hello Godfrey. You remember me then?'

'It's good to see you,' he said effusively. He was incapable of a sarcastic remark hinting at my recent absence from services. 'Coping with the change in season?'

Departing from my custom of obeying protocol, I replied, 'Not so well, this year, as it happens.'

'Ah well,' he said brightly. 'It is only three months until the days start getting longer. And the winter test matches are on the telly now, aren't they?'

'Yes,' I said, somewhat surprised. I was not aware he followed sport closely.

'Colin,' he said in a lower voice, shepherding me a little to one side. 'So glad you're here: I want you to meet someone.'

We stood a moment or two next to two ladies who were chatting breezily. Both had flecks of silver in their dark hair, but one was quite elderly while the other was about my age. Godfrey was far too polite to interrupt but, awaiting his chance, succeeded in attracting the attention of the younger woman, who disengaged herself as soon as courtesy would permit.

'This is Elizabeth, Elizabeth Giles,' he said to me. 'Elizabeth, this is Colin; terrific fellow and a fine opening bat.'

She smiled. It is possible to perceive intelligence in a face; and kindness. I noted both, as well as a most natural reserve. The few lines on her face had added a touch of grace to looks that I assumed had always been fine. Her hair was stylish and quite short, with just a fleck of grey here and there. She wore a smart but very modest blouse and long dark skirt. No make-up, but little need – she possessed the fine complexion of one who lived healthily, together with a faintest hint of sadness at pleasures foregone. I have to say I also was in possession of a little uncertainty at being introduced. I recognised her as the earnest new lady who had been sat near me in the pews, confidently inserting the language of equality into our centuries-old Creed: so '...was made man' became: '... was made human.' And she omitted the word 'virgin' before 'Mary'. Such trendy vocabulary grated with my traditionalist soul, but I did not wish to appear curmudgeonly as well as conservative, so remained polite. The trend-setters liked to call their terminology 'inclusive', but they quite cheerfully excluded the more conventional Christian.

At that point one of the parish council members, whose name I habitually forgot, emerged suddenly and said to the cleric, 'Godfrey, dear, please come and sort out this mess.'

'Do excuse me,' he said politely to us both, and departed.

'So what do you do, Colin?' Elizabeth asked.

'Um, my name isn't Colin, actually, it's Brian, Brian Clarke.'

She laughed out loud. 'Oh dear, is our young vicar here really so absent-minded?'

'No, no, no! Not at all. Colin is a nickname for me. It has been for 15, maybe 20 years. I first met Godfrey at the cricket ground in early summer, which must be where he picked it up. I haven't really worked out how to explain it to him, and it's kind of stuck.'

'What an odd nickname.'

'After Colin Cowdrey. It's quite a compliment to my ability, if not my figure,' I offered, blushing out of a fear that I appeared immodest. 'Colin Cowdrey was …' I began.

'Don't worry,' she replied. 'I know all about cricket, through my family. Godfrey just told me about a new book, I think it's called *Rain Men*, that refers to a vicar who could never walk down the aisle of his church without wondering if it would take spin. What do you think?'

'What? Oh, very funny.'

'No – I was being serious. The aisle here at All Saints, would it favour spin bowlers?'

'No,' I replied. 'Hard, fast and true. Quite a shiny surface. I would go with an all pace attack. Run-ups, however, might pose a problem for a left arm fast bowler from one end, given the position of the font, while the altar would be tricky to negotiate from the other. For a return match at St Peters, however, I would take along a spin bowler or two. There's a nice bit of timber flooring at one end and the polish has worn off.'

There was a pause. I began to feel anxious already. Despite my generally calm exterior, I was invariably more socially insecure than people recognised, and typically convinced that I was a terrible bore to a woman, especially if I was attracted to her. 'Are you new to the, er town?' I asked. Our growing conurbation could have been described as a village when I was young, so I felt uncomfortable with the word 'town'.

'No, I've just moved into the neighbouring parish – St Peters, as it happens. I don't know how many spin bowlers live there. But I know Godfrey from a few years ago and I was anxious to catch up. It's beautiful round here.'

'Is it? Yes, I suppose it is,' I replied. I looked around. I guess it was. The church, solidly Saxon with its square tower, ancient burial ground with gnarled yew trees, drew visitors and admirers from beyond the town. The celebrated common featured our cricket ground, and led on to more expansive woodland just beyond a twinkling brook and a road. A semi-circle of mature silver birches, only a few of which were felled by the great storm of '87, framed an English scene picturesque enough to attract Japanese tourists, who loved to film, especially as a cricket game was in play. For a participant in a keenly fought competitive match in which we concentrate fiercely, it was odd to be forming part of what was, for a visitor, a quaint moving tableau. I often cast my eye proudly at the green fields and woodland that extended from the common, but also nervously, gathering that the developers probably monitored this precious terrain also. For now, the housing estates had been developed steadily on the other side of town, behind the long and winding high street, populated with an array of shops and half a dozen pubs. As the town grew, so did the club: there had been two sides on a Saturday and one on a Sunday when I began in the 1970s; this had become three and two respectively.

'Have you lived here all your life?' she asked.

'Yes. Yes I have. I've never really thought about how beautiful it is. Familiarity and all that, I suppose. I tend to associate the rural scenery with decline. Can't find lost meadows with skylarks any more.'

'Oh, but you can,' she countered brightly. 'Perhaps you have to look harder. I was on the downs yesterday, and I was planning on going again today,' she said. 'There are still enough spires and green fields and woodland to make me believe that we haven't quite ruined God's work.'

'You must have caught your death!' I exclaimed. 'It was a grim day yesterday.'

'Oh no,' she said, looking down briefly and returning her gaze. 'I have my sturdy jacket, waterproof trousers and walking boots. I love the autumn, and to feel the wind through my hair, as if God himself was passing through. Sorry, I'm getting carried away.'

'Not at all,' I ventured. 'I've always regarded the summer as the pinnacle of the year, and neglected the other seasons. Perhaps I should learn to appreciate them.'

'Summer's only short,' she reminded me.

'I know. Sometimes in June and July I long so much for the next one that I can scarcely enjoy the present. Did you know that cuckoos are only in the country for six weeks? They're basically an African species.'

I felt that I was losing my audience. People often thought my presentation of knowledge was conceit when, far more frequently, it was a symptom of nerves – some fact vaguely related to a subject of conversation entered my head and left my lips because it could; because I found that mentally leafing through an encylopaedia to be safer territory than digging even a shallow way into my own emotion, or daring to inquire into another's.

'Indeed. Listen, er, Elizabeth, It's been nice to meet you. I hope to see you again, but I have to be off now.' I tried to smile but it was probably an effort distorted by nerves.

'That would be nice,' she said, turning sedately to rejoin her companion.

I crossed the gravel yard, the yellow leaves swirling around my ankles, conscious of a quickening of the pulse, a surging temperature around my collar and in my cheeks despite the cool air, and a vague sense of guilt that I had departed Elizabeth's company as swiftly as I had, recognising that I had left not because I disliked her company, but rather the opposite. I recall a mildly perplexed look on her face as I departed.

3

Kinetic poetry

It is an unwritten rule of male sports teams (perhaps female ones also) that no one must be called by their real name, unless it is a shortened, lengthened or corrupted version. In short, everyone must have a nickname; at least one. These vary in origin. My nickname, of which I was immensely proud, was either 'Col' or 'Cowdrey' because of an apparent similarity in appearance to the great former England and Kent cricketer, and a similar relish for fast bowling. Tony Bates was known usually as 'Briz', the etymology of which is as follows: he was originally dubbed 'Eric Bristow' or 'Eric' after the famous darts player. This was a sarcastic nickname, because Tony was spectacularly bad at darts, often missing the board completely. Entire drinking parties were known to up and leave their table if it were located anywhere near the contest as he rose from his seat, arrows clutched optimistically in his right hand, and walked towards the oche. 'Eric', however, posed a problem as a nickname, given that we had a real one in the team, so it became 'Bristow', often shortened to 'Briz'.

The real Eric was known as 'Bodger', as in 'Bodge-jobs', because of a reputed amateurishness in his enthusiastic home improvement projects. My understanding was that his skills had improved in recent years; his misfortune was that his most memorable calamity occurred when an entire set of shelves, loaded with records, books and sporting trophies, fell into one another like a pack of cards just before the start of the England-Argentina World Cup quarter final in 1986, when a dozen or so of his mates were gathered on sofas and chairs in the large sitting room of his parents' home, pouring their beers, ready for the match. Everyone agreed that the spectacular collapse was the highlight of the day, given how the wizardry of Diego Maradona on the pitch defeated England's efforts.

Andy Peacock, a young spin bowler, had been known as 'Pike' ever since an epic drinking session in 1989 after we had chased down 230 against Horsham 2nds in a home fixture. Young Andy, just 19 years old at the time, had fallen asleep under the snooker table after several pints and, lain unnoticed, was locked in overnight. His mother was distraught at his non-appearance, but decided to seek out intelligence about the evening's events before alerting the police, and contacted the club skipper and groundsman to arrange a search of the club's premises. The lad was apparently awoken by the sound of the key in the door, bumped his head on the underside of the table before emerging to greet the three of them, at which point his imperious mother declared: 'You stupid boy!' It helped that he resembled his Dad's Army namesake.

The regular first XI of the mid 1990s, in approximate batting order, was: Col, Briz, Hobbit , Del-Boy (or 'Trotter'), Bodger, Kennel, Iron Gloves or Ned, Hurricane or Keano, Sticks, Jock and Pike.

In the scorebook we were listed as Clarke, Hibbert,

Bates, Cooper, Gray, Sprake, Kelly, Keane, Collins, McAllister and Peacock.

Our family called us Brian, Greg, Anthony, Derek, Eric, Hector, Clive, David, Phil, Craig and Andy.

And you thought Russian patronyms were confusing.

The next game was the final one of the season. I had caught up on sleep, a little, between morning service and start of play, dozing on the sofa as my mug of tea cooled slowly on the carpet. It was another home fixture – our ground was so attractive we tended to be popular with visiting sides for friendly games, which peppered the season in between league fixtures. By mid-September, the league had finished. We batted first again. The wind had died down and there was a faint warmth in the autumnal sunshine as I strode out to the crease, as usual taking first strike with Tony at the other end. The pitch exuded its aroma of earth and grass but had dried a little, since the day before. It looked like a good track. For the first time in several days, the air of melancholy lifted. I could enjoy the last rays of summer for the next six hours, and I was determined to score some runs.

My nerves always diminish as the bowler begins his run. An element of control returns, though it is never complete. A batsman cannot determine the delivery that is directed towards him; he can only react. Therein lies the thrill and the fear. You are central, but cannot decide the context. Cricket is full of such paradoxes. It is genteel from afar; gladiatorial in the middle. It is a team game, made up of individual battles. Its ethos encourages generosity of spirit, yet it is clinically ruthless – you cannot muddle through on a bad afternoon like you sometimes can in football or rugby. A game lasts forever, yet a batsman's stay may be over in an instant. Cricket is the slowest game and the fastest game; the most polite and the most unforgiving.

My adversary this afternoon was a lanky youngster with a long run up. The ball landed short. I could see the glistening red and gold orb easily as it kicked up towards my chest. The bounce was true, and I patted it down with ease. The next was shorter still, and wide. I struck the ball cleanly; in the air for a little while, but safely away to the boundary. The bowler, flustered and letting his loss of pride show, ran in even faster and dug the ball in even harder. I saw it early, moved into position quickly, and kept watching. It bounced a little higher than I had expected but, adjusting quickly and following through with a hook shot, connected sweetly and sent it high. It flew over the umpire, over the fielder, and cleared the boundary by some ten feet. That felt good. The hook is the most difficult and satisfying shot to play. It is also dangerous, because to play it properly you have to get your eyes immediately in front of the ball. Only once had I missed and got struck. I had wanted to play on but apparently there was blood. I did not care for the recent trend of donning a helmet, that some of the younger players were starting to, feeling that one would weigh me down and hamper my reactions.

'Pitch it up,' the captain grumbled at his charge, with sufficient irritation for me to detect disunity in the opposing ranks – always an encouraging sign when engaged in a team game. The bowler immediately over-compensated, firing the ball up onto my toes. I moved inside and sent it where it seemed to want to go, which was away to the fine leg boundary and into the twinkling brook that marked the edge of the common. Fourteen off the first four balls! I could hear my team mates cheering and applauding.

I struck a few more during the next few overs, all deliciously off the middle of the bat, until I received one from the young fast bowler which bounced a little more than I had expected. I still made fairly good contact. The ball flew hard and low above the ground towards a spindly youth in the field who stretched out a hand into which the ball stuck; almost as if it had decided to rest there, rather than being deliberately obstructed by any human intention. I stood for a moment, stupefied. 'This could not happen,' I explained to myself. 'I am far too good for these players. That fielder is not capable of catching a bus. The rules should be changed.' I looked about myself, quickly apprehending that the eleven men around me were not about to concede a change or exemption to the rules, tucked the bat under my armpit, and began to tug the gloves from my hands as I walked away. By the time I reached the pavilion I was smiling to myself: 38 at better than a run a ball, and I felt better still as the afternoon wore on. Such a quick scoring rate at the start of the innings helped us build a good total. In the field, I took a smart catch, low to my left, at second slip (Colin Cowdrey's fielding position) as 'Hurricane' Keane ran through their top order.

We won comfortably, and I could feel satisfied with my contribution. Such a short cameo can be more pleasurable than a long, grafting innings, and the memory of that six would keep me warm on many a winter's evening. The kinetic poetry of a perfectly timed shot; the surprise and satisfaction as it flies off the sweetest of spots, requiring less effort to send the ball further when the timing is *just* right, forms a physical memory that begins in the body but takes up residence in the mind. Such sublime instances are like moments in music. How limited in reflection are those philistine Darwinists who have colonised our narratives of life, insisting that all human behaviour can be reduced to mere purpose; that achievement, harmony, inspiration or endeavour are just means to an end to impress or gain advantage. The moments in which we are most alive; most conscious of our aliveness, have no function – they just are.

Perhaps not every batsman thinks like this after hitting a six.

4

Lost

'Last game of the season – great win,' said Derek. 'Let's have an extra jug!'

He was often wanting to keep the party going – or at any rate avoid going home. I attempted to put myself in a sociable mood but, while the joy of the win was genuine, I felt vaguely restless and the conversation quickly palled. 'I've got to go,' I explained.

'What already?' he asked, disappointed but not disapproving. 'Oh well. I'll see you at the club dinner, if not before.'

The other team mates offered friendly good-byes and I dragged my kit bag out of the pavilion and across the car park behind. The sun had disappeared, and a strengthening wind had brought some menacing clouds. At the far end there stood a woman appearing somewhat ill at ease as she looked about her. I recognised Elizabeth immediately, in spite of her casual dress.

'Hello again!' I announced.

'Oh, hello Colin, er, Brian, I mean,' she replied.

'What brings you here?' I asked.

'I've just been for a walk, and I was disorientated for a moment,' she looked down at her map, sealed in a plastic transparent holder that hung from her neck. 'No; I've worked it out now. I parked the car next to a green, but it must be Parsons Green, on the other side of town; not this one. I must have taken the wrong fork in the woods.'

'That's half a mile away, I'm afraid,' I said. 'I'll accompany you there, if you like.'

'That would be nice. What about your kit bag?'

'Oh, I'll leave it in the pavilion. I can pick it up tomorrow.'

I returned immediately. 'Are you warm enough?' I asked. The wind had picked up and the sun had disappeared.

'Oh, yes, this jacket is impenetrable,' she said. 'Let's hope we miss the shower.'

'It'll be a heavy one, I think,' I said. The edge of the cloud directly above us was pale grey and ragged but its heart, only a little further away, was dark and low.

'Did you win?' she asked, as we began walking, first along the edge of the common and then on a residential street towards the town centre.

'Yes, quite comfortably actually,' I explained.

'How many did you score, then?'

'Thirty-eight. Should have had more.'

'Is that it for the season, now?'

'Yes. It's rather poignant,' I said, but in a light tone of voice, attempting a little self-mockery.

'How do you occupy yourself in the winter?'

'I am mostly sedentary: reading, chess, pubs. Pub quizzes, though I play squash to keep fit. People describe them as middle-aged habits but the truth is I've always followed them. I detested rock music or discotheques when I was young.'

'You're in the prime of your life now, then,' she suggested.

I paused. 'Yes,' I began. 'I suppose I am. I've never really thought of it in that way.' The rain began to spit and trickle down our faces. 'What about you?' I asked.

'Well, a kindred spirit in some ways,' she said, though in an unemotional way. 'Well, I like a bit of rock and roll, if you count Joni Mitchell and Simon & Garfunkel; but also a sense of, well, vocation – though that tends to waver, these days,' she sounded quite apologetic; whether the reticence was as to her admission of faith or her subsequent doubt, was unclear.

Without the rain, I might have lacked the confidence to inquire, but as it began to get heavier, I dared ask: 'Would you care to join me for a drink? We're quite near the Swan, which is a lovely pub.'

Rather to my surprise, she did not hesitate at all. 'That'd be lovely.'

The shower rapidly became a torrent and we became quite wet in the 100 yards of so of the walk, though Elizabeth was better clad in her walking jacket. Even though it was only September, the landlord had lit a fire – it was generally good for business – and we gratefully sat near it, on small stools at a circular wooden table. I ordered the drinks and joined her. She had an orange juice and I had ordered a pint of beer. The condensation on the cold glass made it stick to the beer mat. I made a note to separate them each time I lifted the glass, sensing this was important and to make a fool of myself was to be avoided.

'So, your, um, sense of vocation then...' I prompted as I sat down, fidgeting with nerves.

'I was a nun,' she explained.

'Oh, I'm sorry, I didn't realise you'd been a....er, I mean.'

She laughed. 'You were going to say "a Catholic",' she alleged. 'I'll let you into a secret: the Church of England has nuns too.'

'Oh, I know, well, I was vaguely aware. Why... er, I mean, how was it?'

'Fine, really fine. I've no regrets. Of course, it was meant to be for life,' she fell silent abruptly. It would be quite wrong to state that her voice 'trailed off'.

Elizabeth tapped her glass with the nail of her little finger as she cast her eyes downwards. The crucifix dangling from a slender silver necklace rocked like a cradle on her throat. 'I really hope it wasn't just a phase. That wouldn't do.'

'There are many ways of serving,' I offered, feeling pathetic.

'I know,' she said simply. 'Still, what about you?'

'Not so devout at all, I confess. Indeed; very little to relate at all. It's just been lately that I've begun to wonder on the purpose of it all. When I was young,' I continued. 'I thought it was those with families who led the routine and purposeless lives. They sought a good education; and for what? To get a good job, good home, and then have children - and then made sure that the children had a good education, good job, good home, and so on. This cycle; this endless repetition seemed to be living life like a Russian doll. I didn't want it. But now I can't see what I rejected it for.'

'Well, you weren't ready then but, well – you're not exactly old,' she said, encouragingly.

There was an awkward silence, of the kind the English are good at. 'So you never wanted to have babies?' she asked.

'Babies, yes. But they have a tendency to grow into children. And the way modern children are supposed to be allowed to run riot and run the show is a scandal. I have a friend who's a hotel proprietor who won't allow them any more at weddings. They run round the place and knock on all the doors and behave like vandals.'

I scolded myself inwardly; how could I possibly form a

favourable impression by admitting a difficulty with children? I softened the tone abruptly. 'What I mean to say is, I always used to wonder in amazement at how a baby, this little miracle, this gift from God, with its air of wisdom and wide-eyed sense of wonder at the beautiful world around him, could transform itself into a rather selfish, whiny creature just running about. Maybe I just happened to stumble upon a particularly bad toddlers' party once.' Another pause. 'I'm sorry, I must sound terribly selfish.'

'No, Colin. People don't have children out of altruism, mostly.'

'Er, Brian,' I said, pedantically. I added: 'I would probably have been a good Dad in the old days, when parents had their own space and children didn't rule the roost, if that doesn't sound too authoritarian.'

'Actually no,' she replied. 'Some family counsellors are beginning to agree that Mum and Dad should do their own thing some of the time, and not devote all their leisure time to entertaining the kids.'

'I guess most things come back into fashion some day.'

'Look,' she said, suddenly appearing nervous. 'I've been prying too much, haven't I? Let's talk about something else.'

'The weather?' I suggested, squeezing some drops of liquid from the sleeve of my sweater.

She laughed.

'How do you know Godfrey?' I asked.

'We were on a retreat together, about five years ago, on Holy Island. It was a "silent" retreat, though we never stopped nattering. Even sneaked out to the pub one night. He was very kind to me. I was going through a very bad time and he seemed the only one to notice. It seemed too good to be true when I got a job so close to his parish.'

'What do you do?'

'I'm a school teacher. English and R.E. I'm surprised you didn't guess. Most people do.'

'There's so much more to someone than their profession, though you wouldn't believe it to hear so much polite conversation. Dinner party talk.'

'Do you go to many dinner parties?'

'No; not any more. I don't fit in - being single, and I'm tired of - I don't know - conversations that are about establishing your status. The trouble is, I fear it has become just one more thing I've given up without filling the void.' I paused for a while to gather my thoughts. 'The thing is,' I continued. 'That I can make all sorts of terribly clever critiques of contemporary fashions, but if it just means I feel alienated from people, then I doubt I have done myself many favours. Or them.'

'It depends entirely on whether these critiques of yours are genuinely what you believe, Colin.'

'Brian.'

'Right. If you believe in them, people will respect you and those worth knowing will want to know you.'

'It's so much easier to cave in.'

'It's not a choice between caving in and rebelling; it's a case of deciding what is genuinely your belief.'

She was gentle in her sureness. We talked at length, I becoming somewhat merry with my pints of beer while she stayed religiously sober in view of her drive home and probably, I supposed, a natural inclination towards temperance. I did not feel sure if the prolonged conversation was because she liked my company or out of desire to stay by the fire, but she seemed at ease.

'Let me give you a lift home,' she offered at the end of the evening.

'It's hardly worth the effort as I live so close,' I said. 'And it's stopped raining.'

'No, I insist. You've been most kind.'

There was silence in the few minutes the journey took, which was odd given the animation of our conversation in the pub. I hoped the fumes from my beery breath were not too unpleasant for her in the small interior.

'Right just before the common, then left.' I said.

'You're handy for the ground, then,' she commented.

'Backs onto it,' I said proudly, grinning like a child. I opened the door and put one step on the raised pavement, before pausing. I felt a little agitated and unsure of myself. 'Um, thank-you for a nice evening,' I said and, with a sudden and unwonted haste, turned briefly to her before alighting fully. I caught a kind expression and heard a brief 'Likewise: 'bye,' before I strode down the short garden path.

5

Contact details

'Hello, Colin?' My attention was called as I walked past the churchyard, on the way back from the newsagent.

'Oh, hello, Godfrey,' I replied. 'How are you?'

'Fine, I'm glad you called by. Could I pick your brains over this boundary dispute. You wouldn't have a minute, would you?'

'Er, yes. Last I heard they were going to concede the extra metre.' This related to a tedious dispute between a developer and the church over the interpretation of some ancient deeds and similarly ancient maps. I had suggested Godfrey take it up with the church's solicitors, but he seemed to prefer my informal advice, being both more accessible and free.

He offered me a cup of dreadfully weak coffee after we entered the rectory, still positioned traditionally next to the church, and not yet sold off, as was becoming the custom. I winced as I took a sip. As far as I could see from the correspondence and the documents, the matter appeared to be sorted, so it was not at all clear that my presence was needed. I suddenly became fixated with Godfrey's nasal hair, which had always been bad but seemed to have sprouted anew. We were sat opposite each other across a small desk in the vicar's administrative office. I noticed for the first time there were similar clumps emerging from his ears, like the thick concentrations of grass in an un-weeded border. His wiry, prematurely grey eyebrows could have picked up radio signals.

'You could at least get it trimmed,' I thought, then suddenly realised from his expression of puzzlement that I had said this out loud.

'Trimmed?!' he inquired.

'Um, the grass. Near the fence. It sometimes helps with cases like this.' I began to sweat.

'Yes,' he said, as though attempting to convince himself. 'I suppose it would. You are most thorough. You think of everything.'

'That's what we're trained for,' I said, nervously.

'Well, that's business. So how are you, Colin? Are you coping any better with the autumnal blues?'

'Not sure – too early to tell. I'm not sure whether autumnal depression is a childhood fixation I should have grown out of by now.'

'Hah!' he said. 'I rather think those are the only fixations we can't grow out of. Don't worry, I'm sure I can find you an interesting sub-committee of the parish council in which to absorb yourself and pass the winter hours.'

'Most generous,' I replied, returning his gentle sarcasm.

'I just wondered - I've realized I don't have your home phone number. Still getting round the new parish.'

'Of course,' I replied, puzzled at his earnest manner given the trivial nature of his request. I scribbled my number on a sheet of paper offered, and added my address for good measure. He wrote simply 'Colin' next to it. I decided to postpone an explanation of my real name once more, fearful of mutual embarrassment.

'My friend Elizabeth says she had a most agreeable meeting with you on Sunday,' he said.

'Oh fine. Yes, I helped her find her car and we had a drink on Sunday evening,' I said hurriedly, as if I had something to confess.

'You and I should have a drink some time,' he said.

'I'm in the Swan every Saturday evening.'

'Maybe this week, then,' he offered.

'See you there.'

'Bye, then.'

'Yes. Bye.'

Odd, I thought. But then Godfrey was odd. He had an air about him, which was deceptive, of appearing distracted, perhaps due to his rarely making eye contact. Parishioners would think he had scarcely listened to a request, as he stood apparently only half listening, looking above them, and scratching his thin wispy hair as if searching for a hat, only to find it honoured the next week. In a similar fashion he would give the impression of naivety when listening to an individual's problems, while at the end of the testimony make a most acute observation.

I was still reflecting on his eccentric manners the next day at work, when I wasn't thinking of the charming and enigmatic Elizabeth. The work was not captivating. I was handling a protracted divorce; not particularly acrimonious but replete with bureaucratic overload given that the couple had set up and run a business together, had three children in fee-paying schools, and two properties, one in France. My office had green leather, like a padded cell, and black mahogany. I swivelled gently in the heavy chair. It was quiet and safe. I had many havens, but rarely a cause to seek refuge. I generally had little impetus to work hard, even, given the wealth and indifference of the partners. The clock ticked. A car passed by the front. Every minute passed with deliberation. I played with my pen as I recalled the conversation with Elizabeth on the previous Sunday; became concerned that I must have appeared rather old-fashioned and boorish, and wondered whether she may wish to continue the acquaintance.

I left the office early and drove out of the tiny car park behind the office, which, as you have probably imagined, was a converted, turreted Victorian mansion of asymmetrical design and imprecise dimensions, in which one constantly suspected the existence of unknown rooms. I waited at the exit as a youth drove a hideously coloured sports car along the short high street at an unpleasant speed, turning heads, including, to my shame, mine. Two school children had begun to cross the road but retreated hurriedly. The driver scarcely slowed, and almost removed their toes as he passed. I muttered beneath my breath, waited for them to cross, and pulled out with exaggerated caution.

The phone was ringing as I entered home - a most uncommon event outside of the cricket season. I reached it before it stopped.

'Hello?'

'Hello, Colin?'

'Er, yes.'

'It's Elizabeth.'

'Hello. It's very nice to hear from you.'

'I hope I'm not disturbing you.'

'Not at all.'

'Godfrey gave me your number. I hope you don't mind.'

'I don't mind at all. It's nice to hear from you.'

'I just wanted to thank you for helping me find my car, and wondered if you wanted to meet again. I'm still new to the area and it's great to make new friends.'

'Well, I would love to.'

'Well as you know, I'm a keen walker along with many of the new friends I've made around here. You mentioned that you're not sure if there is nice countryside left these days, and I've discovered there are some beautiful spots in the past few weeks. So would you care to come for a walk this coming weekend?'

'A walk?' I said, betraying surprise, and probably sounding ill-mannered. I gave myself a scolding. 'Where to?'

She chuckled. 'Well, not *to* anywhere; just up on the downs. Enjoy the views and the fresh air.'

I had never considered such an enterprise before. 'Oh, sure,' I said, trying to sound casual, and caught by conflicting emotions. On the one hand, I had never before understood 'a walk' to be entertainment in itself but I was also, I noticed, excited at the prospect of meeting her again. Was this an invitation on – dare I say it – a 'date'?

She hastily added: 'If you would rather not, don't feel obliged...' She sounded oddly nervous, considering her apparent aplomb at the previous encounter.

'No, that sounds wonderful. Should I bring stout boots and sensible clothes?'

'Well I think so,' she said, sounding more comfortable. 'Unless you'd prefer dancing shoes.'

'They're rather worn through, I'm afraid.'

She gave me a meeting point and time, precise and confident as though she were the local and not the newcomer.

Now, I said to myself; it couldn't be a date, could it? Just a walk. But then, *she* had called *me*. What would I wear?

How would I conduct myself? My imagination had already begun to fire. In fine weather, a romantic stroll through plots of beechen green, a faintly warm autumnal sun making delicate patterns of light and shade on her face. Our hands brush together, then clutch each other; with increasing confidence, we begin to embrace.... No, I'm getting ahead of myself. She probably invited me out of Christian charity, sensing my loneliness. I felt anxious and excited, torn between getting my hopes up and not getting my hopes up – both options generating a tumultuous mixture of insecurity and anxiety. Why was I fretting? Why did it suddenly all matter so much?

6

Up on the Downs

In the end, I did get my hopes up. I had gone to bed early and slept well. I breakfasted in style that Saturday morning, having prepared eggs and bacon accompanied with hot tea and buttered toast. The morning was bright, and I was able to open the French windows and let the fresh damp smell of turf and autumnal leaves, drying slowly in the weak sunshine, waft in from the garden as I ate and read the newspaper. The recollection of Elizabeth's keen friendliness on the phone, and the consciousness that the initiative had been hers, prompted me to permit the awakening of desire.

I even spent a while getting ready. I had sports shoes that were suitable for walking on the downs, and took some time to clean them. I had had my hair trimmed the day before; that morning I spent additional time shaving and trimming stray nasal hairs and ironing my most casual shirt (which wasn't very casual). I even added a dash of cologne. I could appear quite handsome, I reflected, in an old-fashioned way, depending on which mirror I used. I was in possession of a hunting jacket in good condition. Would a Harris tweed flat cap be too aristocratic, I wondered? I folded it up and placed it inside the inside jacket pocket, to be held in reserve. A shower of rain would be sufficient excuse.

I found the meeting point easily enough, and arrived punctually, having found a space to park by the green of the tiny village nearby. The rendezvous point was by a stile opposite a country pub, underneath a mildly mildewed and rotting wooden signpost bearing the indented legend PUBLIC FOOTPATH, tilted slightly downwards and a little askew but with sufficient honesty towards a grassy path the other side of the stile, bordered by high hedgerow on the one side and a ploughed field on the other. I saw Elizabeth straight away and walked towards her. She looked cheerful, and greeted me warmly. There was, however, another group of walkers there, all dressed in regulation green waterproofs and stout boots, chattering as they looked at their Ordnance Survey maps. They congregated with quite inappropriate proximity to Elizabeth and me, I felt, but otherwise there seemed little to dent my hopes for the day. After a minute or so of polite chat, however, during which Elizabeth assured me she had had an agreeable week, was in good health and planned to visit our church again before long, she was approached by a tall, eager white-haired gentleman from the group. 'Excuse me, Elizabeth, just wanted to ask if you're coming to the meeting next month on campaigning against the debt crisis?'

I rapidly absorbed the humiliating truth. This was no personal invitation to me, and the physical sensation of joy that I had permitted to rise in my breast was punctured. It fell as a leaden weight to become the familiar feeling of drudgery located somewhere near to that part of the stomach known as its pit. There were about seven of them; all earnest-looking older people, pacing about and chatting.

It got worse. The earnest campaigner turned and gave me a steady gaze, as Elizabeth said to him: 'Martin, this is Colin – Colin, Martin.'

I did not bother to correct her by asserting my real name. I anticipated I would have little inclination to become acquainted with this seemingly intrusive individual, though I confess that at that point his mere presence was an irritation. In any case, he confirmed my instinct by officiously demanding of me: 'Hello Colin, will *you* be supporting the campaign to have Third World debt cancelled?'

He asked this in a rather pointed fashion, as though I had volunteered the conversational topic myself, or invited myself into a discussion. 'Well,' I began. 'Default can pose problems for poorer countries and the problem is often corruption and poor governance in Africa.'

'So, you blame the African nations for the effects of colonialism?' he said, rather aggressively, I thought.

'No, I….'

He marched off to join the other group, shaking his head. I turned to Elizabeth and protested: 'I was criticising the rich elite, not the ordinary people,' I said to her. 'I fear he's misunderstood me completely. I thought we were going on a walk, not a march.' I looked down and kicked some leaves and dirt, scuffing the sports shoes that I had spent so long cleaning, and immediately felt guilty that my bad temper was aggravating the situation.

Elizabeth was apologetic and mildly embarrassed, and said: 'Sorry, I should have explained how it's a regular hiking group, mostly church-goers. I'm afraid Martin gets rather carried away with his causes. We can talk about anything you want. It is a friendly group on the whole; I'm still something of a newcomer myself.'

I walked by her side as we set off, trying to recover my spirits and at least put on a show of friendliness that belied my renewed pessimism. 'I've never really done this, you know; well not as an activity in its own right,' I said, getting into my stride. We walked on a few paces. 'Aaah,' I said taking deep cool breaths and gazing at the golden, green and brown view. 'Very autumnal.'

'Quite remarkable, really,' she quipped. 'This time of year.'

'Ah well,' I said. 'It does sometimes come as a shock, our summer is so short.'

We reached a stile over which she stepped quickly, with deft movements, slim and girl-like in her cords and thick jacket, before waiting my more ponderous progress. She was delicate in manner and astonishingly light of foot, as though regretting that she had to press her negligible weight upon God's earth at all. We were entering some woodland as the path veered and took us gently upwards towards the downs.

'Do you play any golf when the cricket season ends?' she asked as we continued walking.

I snorted. 'Hitting a stationary ball? It's about as exciting as picking up litter.'

'A good walk ruined,' she commented.

'Yes, and I don't even ...' I interrupted my dreadful gaffe hurriedly, but too late, and felt my face turning crimson. Fortunately, she was still a little ahead of me. 'I mean,' I added desperately. 'I'm not accustomed to walking. This is marvellous, though. I've lived in this area all my life and probably never walked on this exact path.'

'I'll be your guide,' she said, and we walked on in silence. I felt uncomfortable, but she seemed rapt and content. I even heard her humming.

We reached a straight, slightly upward path of dead leaves.

Heavy old trees stood warily on either side, but to the left only for a short way. Just beyond, a faded timber and barbed wire fence marked the edge of the woods, below which the ground fell abruptly to a grassy hollow of vivid green. Ahead of us and above us was a straight fence and in the middle a stile, like a knot in a taut string. We reached it and squelched in a patch of mud, entering another stretch of woodland before the open downs. It was steep for a while and I was a little short of breath.

She was silent for a minute or two. Ah well, if she will never meet me again, I had best enjoy this day. I wasn't sure that country walking quite captivated me, as an activity in itself, but I enjoyed Elizabeth's company, and hoped to continue escaping the others', though I had little confidence that she cared much care for mine. Her next question took me quite by surprise. 'Do you believe in miracles?'

'Yes,' I replied, after a pause. 'Especially the miracle in the every-day. Life is a miracle. Everything's a miracle.'

At that moment a bird with a heavily undulating flight swooped right in front of us, and perched on the rotting carcass of a dying oak stump to our right, just four or five yards away, only a few feet above the ground. 'A woodpecker!' Elizabeth exclaimed.

'Yes!' I replied. 'Oh, he's magnificent. Isn't he handsome?'

'Yes – *gorgeous*.' He flew off. She looked up at me, inquisitorially, playfully, with a little smile.

'I haven't seen one for a while, actually,' I added. 'He was magnificent – stunning plumage.'

'Always "he", I notice,' she said, playfully. 'Why can't an animal be a she?'

'Because he has a red patch on the back of his head. On the adult female, that part is black.'

'Oh.'

It was a nice victory, though I had to try not to smirk. There was a pause, more comfortable than the last one – for me at least.

'So, miracles. Do you believe in them?' she continued. 'It's the thing atheists always throw at me. I mean, real miracles, not just the colouring on a woodpecker. Divine interventions. Angels.'

Impulsively, I replied: 'Actually, I am an angel.'

'Are you, now?' she asked, with mock seriousness. 'Which category – Guardian?'

'Fallen,' I replied. 'Well, more like kicked out, if I'm honest.'

'Oh, dear.'

'Yes, I failed the trumpet audition.'

'I guess the examination must be difficult.'

'It was. There was that – and one or two of what were termed "moral lapses". I guess flirting with Mary Magdalene at the Christmas party was a mistake, with hindsight. It didn't go unnoticed.'

'Do all fallen angels get sent to rural mid-Sussex?'

'Mostly. The really bad ones end up in Hove.'

She giggled. I hadn't been sure she was capable of a girlish chuckle and, given that I had assumed that she would not want to see me again after that day, I hadn't really been worrying about her reaction.

'Once when I was a teenager,' she recalled. 'I was at a party. I hadn't so much as kissed a boy. Anyway, this slightly older, quite handsome guy took a shine to me. We got chatting, and he began kissing me. I expected to be shocked but I was surprised at how much I enjoyed it. He took me by the hand and led me out of the house. It was a warm summer evening and we were heading up to the woods. I was terribly naïve; I really thought that all he wanted to do was more kissing. Anyway, this stranger in a pale suit appeared and distracted him. He seemed to know him. There was something that the stranger whispered in the lad's ear to cause him to let go of my hand and depart, waving me a brief goodbye. I watched him walk down the street. Then I turned round and the stranger was gone. I learned later that the boy who started to seduce me was a real bad guy – left several girls in the lurch, with their hearts broken, at least one of them pregnant.'

'Your guardian angel, protecting your virtue. You must have felt enormous relief and gratitude?'

'Yes,' she replied. 'But worse than that, I also had a twinge of regret.'

There was more to this Elizabeth than met the eye.

'Have you ever married?' she asked suddenly, but with such grace I scarcely felt my privacy was compromised.

'No,' I ventured, after a pause.

'I'm sorry, I ask too many questions.'

'No, no! I don't mind at all. I'm flattered by the interest.'

'Has there been anyone close?'

I looked up at her and thought of Brigid. 'Just one,' I replied. 'We were going to marry.'

'If it's too painful, Colin, please change the subject.'

'No, not at all. It was sad but not tragic. She's happily married now, with three children, and we're still in touch. It just wasn't to be. Aunty Kath was still alive when we were seeing each other, and I felt a little embarrassed to be still living with her. I was already into my 30s. We were going to marry, but it all felt vaguely contrived; you know, Mary was a friend of a friend of the family; and we were of the same age, and well-intentioned people put us together. Marriage seemed like something we ought to do, and the relationship just ran out of puff.'

'That's so sad.'

'I was maybe too private, as well. It was difficult to be with someone who would make so many comments on me - even on the little things I did, like how I made the tea or mowed the lawn. I began feeling, "I don't want this person in my life". Also, she talked frequently about starting a family. I just had an image of being knee-deep in nappies and screaming toddlers.'

Elizabeth stayed silent at this point and I worried immediately that I had said this too sharply. I tried changing the subject: 'She didn't really approve of cricket at all; thought men should give up silly sports once they got married – or certainly once they had children. And cricket is so very time-consuming – I would have had the choice of playing fewer games, being laden with guilt, or giving up, when it's such a big part of my life. She could also be sharp-tongued at times, also. She would often say things like "Well you'll never believe what so-and-so has done" when the poor chap in question had not done much at all really. She used to make such quick judgements on people. I do prefer people who wait until their opinion is asked for.'

'That must be overbearing if you're used to your own company,' commented Elizabeth. She said this gently but also gave the impression of being a little wary; choosing her vocabulary with care.

I continued, 'Mary even once said something like "Your Aunt Kath is such a gossip!" which I did think was rather poor judgement and harsh. It was Aunt Kath who raised me. She was the sweetest person imaginable.'

Elizabeth paused for a long while. Finally she asked, 'Have you ever been jealous, since she married?'

'No, because you see it was I who ended it. So seeing her happy now is a blessed relief.'

We walked on further, the ground becoming a shade drier as we reached higher ground. 'What about you?' I dared to ask at length.

'Mmm?' she inquired.

'Have you, I mean, has there been anyone close?'

'No, well not really.'

'Not *really*?' I asked. I was astonished at such ambiguous phrasing from someone who had appeared so clear and frank until that point.

'Long story,' she added, a little colour in her cheek. 'I'm sorry if I sound evasive, or defensive.'

'No need to apologize,' I said, respectfully but feeling somewhat confused. 'Defensive' was a word I employed in relation to chess or cricket, not conversations or relationships. 'I won't press for details,' I added gently.

'I'd love to tell you, Colin. Some other day.'

Another one of the walkers caught up with us and invited herself into our conversation. I felt irritated and jealous, but tried to stay courteous. Fortunately, they became engaged in talk about matters and people I did not know, permitting me to become lost in my thoughts. Was there anything now to look forward to, ever? A pub quiz next week, the cricket club dinner and the batting award, then Christmas, to be followed by the inexorable physical and mental decline towards death.

We entered some dense woods at the top of the hill, and the path disappeared. Elizabeth consulted with some of the others and they concluded that we were not far from where the cars were parked, but it looked unfamiliar. I playfully kicked some leaves around, peering through the trees for a sight of the valley and a reference point. Within a few minutes, we had arrived back at the village that lay close to the pub from which we started, arriving at a green near a war memorial.

The white and grey stone obelisk bore a disturbingly lengthy list for such a tiny village, some 15 names. We paused and watched, to pay respects.

'Such a dreadful waste,' said Elizabeth. Her friend, to whom I had not been introduced, nodded briefly.

'Cut down in their prime – such brave lads,' I said. 'But for an accident of birth .... our generation was lucky.'

'The second war had a just cause – against the Nazis. But these poor guys from 1914-18 were just pawns in power plays by the great powers. It was a crime,' she spoke with unexpected force, contrasting with her customary gentleness.

'Mmm,' I said. 'It wasn't so different.'

'What do you mean?'

'The British declared war in 1939 because the Nazi forces invaded Poland. In 1914 it was because the Kaiser's army invaded Belgium. Britain was duty-bound to defend Belgium, having set it up as a neutral country after the Napoleonic wars.'

'Really? I didn't know that.' Elizabeth replied with genuine interest, though her friend drifted away.

I felt nervous, sensing a political argument of a type I disliked – which was most kinds. I hated disagreeing with someone I cared about, or someone I was getting to know. I opted for a less contentious observation. 'They must have been scared. Many said they knew on the morning of the battle if there was going to be a bullet or a whizz-bang with their name on it.'

'Are you scared of death?' she asked, slightly taking me by surprise.

'Oh God, no.'

'Why not?'

'Well, I never really expected to be born – that came as a surprise. And think of the things I wouldn't have to worry about any more: violence, hooliganism, ecological degradation, hideous TV presenters, tabloid newspapers, housing estates on the green belt. Do you get scared?'

'Since I turned 40, yes,' she said. 'I'm terrified there may be nothing. When I was young and sure of my faith, I just knew I would meet Jesus. Now, I'm not so sure.'

'You can't worry about a crisis of faith, can you? If you don't have doubt from time to time, you can't experience faith.'

'OK,' she replied.

7

Remembering Lawrence Rowe

'Do you think the French are more intelligent than us?' asked Hector. It was the night of our regular pub quiz. He, Graham and Jane and I formed the regular team for the monthly competition. Jane helped us with 'girly' subjects like horticulture and food and drink but also, being a maths teacher and exceptionally well read, was probably the single strongest asset to the team. She possessed an astonishingly quick eye for anagrams, which occasionally the quizmaster tested us with on a written round.

It was hard to know how to reply to Hector's opening conversational gambit. His eccentric way of thinking prompted some unexpected lines of inquiry. On other occasions, he had asked if intelligent alien life forms were likely to play sport, if Mikhail Gorbachev had planned the end of Communism, and whether gravity was universal. Our considered replies to the first two were respectively: Hopefully not, as it's a whole new way for England to lose at cricket; and Unlikely, but plausible. Graham gave a lengthy reply to the last question which we sensed was comprehensive and authoritative, though neither Hector nor I could follow it in the slightest. One feared Hector would be prone to belief in conspiracy theories, given his often unusual take on the news, but he always stayed on the right side of sanity, tending to exhibit genuine curiosity rather than paranoid projections about puzzling or difficult events.

'Well, I'm not sure you can conclude whether an entire nation is more or less intelligent, collectively, than another,' I said in reply. 'They have produced some impressive writers and philosophers, I guess.'

'Also they speak French. French is difficult.'

'Well, not if you're French …'

'Yes, but it's so fluent and they speak so quickly. English is a bit clunky, by comparison.'

'Our sense of inferiority probably dates back to Norman times, when the aristocrats spoke French and we spoke Anglo-Saxon,' I said. 'That's why your average English bloke thinks it's a bit "poncey" to pronounce French words correctly. Inverted snobbery, really.'

Graham observed: 'George Orwell once wrote that, in 1914 a million English men went abroad for the first time in their lives and came back with a loathing of all foreigners, except the Germans.'

'Quite,' I said. 'Distant cousins.'

'Except most of them didn't come back,' said Hector.

'Actually,' I replied, 'most of them did, though many were badly injured. Around a third of servicemen lost their lives in the Great War. So two thirds survived.'

Hector gave me a perplexed look but seemed to accept the opinion, furrowing his brow beneath his dark, matted hair and stooping to drink his beer with an abrupt movement, like that of a heron taking a frog.

The quizmaster handed out the questions. First of all, there was a picture quiz. The subject was 'music', by which, of course, they meant 'pop and rock music'. I had given up protesting at this prejudice on the part of quizmasters. We were handed a sheet of ten photocopied black and white images of 'stars', with their outlandish clothing and extraordinary hair. Teasingly, knowing that I would have little clue as to the identity of any, they asked me to identify one. I pointed to the picture of a pale young man with straight long hair playing an electric guitar and suggested 'Jimi Hendrix.' They laughed.

'Why is that so obviously wrong?'

'Because,' pointed out Hector. 'Jimi Hendrix was left-handed.'

'Right,' I replied nervously, not completely convinced. They were still tittering.

In the next rounds the questions were read out. We had a lucky draw with subjects: sport, history, politics, general knowledge. Everyone pitched in and with the running score kept updated verbally at frequent intervals, we knew that we were near the top throughout the evening. After the final points were tallied (Hector knew every single one of the pop stars in the photographs – he was an avid fan of all sorts of bands and singers; he was good on movies, too) we were tied for first place with another team. There was to be a tie-break. The quizmaster pulled the subject matter out of a hat. 'Sport,' she declared. 'It goes straight to sudden death. I ask a question. If only one team gets it right, they are the winners. If neither or both get it right, I ask another. And so on.'

Each team could confer, hand the answer on a written piece of paper to the quizmaster.

'A cricket question,' she announced. Hector and I looked hopeful. 'Which West Indies batsman scored a century and a double century on his test match debut, and later in his career scored a triple century in a test match?'

A big, smug grin spread across my face. 'Too easy,' I said. Hector looked up, frustrated that he didn't know. 'You know the answer?'

'Yup,' I replied. We whispered in conference and I wrote down the name swiftly, handing it to the quizmaster.

The other team's answer was read out first. 'Clive Lloyd. Incorrect.' Then mine – or rather, ours: 'Lawrence Rowe. This is the correct answer. So the team Eccentrics wins.'

My team mates cheered. 'Of course,' said Hector. 'I remember him now. Classy player.'

'He was,' I said. 'He got 70-odd when Sir Viv got 291 at the Oval in '76. I went to two days of that game. Fantastic play. I failed the Norman Tebbit cricket test that week, I must admit. I was cheering on the Windies!'

'Dennis Amiss played well, though.'

'Yes, real courage. Superb.'

It was an enjoyable evening, although at that point, in the moment of celebrating our win, I ordered another pint of beer, my fourth, which proved with hindsight to be a mistake. I recall visiting the gents just before heading home and becoming guiltily aware of a slight stagger after I had closed the door behind me, and I was forced to cling to the cold white enamel of a hand basin to steady myself. I took deep breaths, trying not to panic, and just calm myself. This was new. There had been a time when I could handle four pints quite easily; now it seemed to make me rather drunk.

I awoke in the small hours, able to recollect little of the conversation towards the end of the evening. I live alone, so I could put on the light, get up, make myself a cup of tea; put music on even, as my large house is not close to the neighbours'. None of these palliatives lessened the renewed feeling of despair; the echoey loneliness of the large house with its sombre furnishings and politely subdued carpeting. Might I be cheered in a modern apartment with bountiful natural light, bright colours and even – heretical thought – cheery pop music by The Beatles or Abba? I shuddered. Had it really come to that?

8

The beautiful Russian doll

I returned to bed and slept for another hour or so. When I awoke fully it was still early. I noted with sadness how much darker for the hour it was than it had been of late. There was no milk in the fridge, and the metal container outside the front door was empty. I reminded myself to inquire after Tony, my batting partner and the milkman, before dressing and heading for the local store.

On the threshold it took a moment for the cold to penetrate. I took a deep breath of metallic air, which tasted the same as on an identical November day of white-grey skies and motionless trees, now nearly stripped of foliage, some 30 years earlier, and felt the same pang of desire for the spring that was still so far off. The crows were noisy in the common, cawing with vigour and swooping from tree to ground and back with the air of proprietors. A toddler, buttoned and scarfed to the neck, ran and leapt behind a mother pushing a pram.

The hockey pitch was kicked up and rough, spreading its dark stain onto a section of the outfield, an incursion against which I protested at every annual general meeting, without success. The cricket square, soft and green behind its sloping, protective fence of timber and chicken wire, sulked.

Every winter I treasure a memory of the early summer, which finds its cherished place through a sense of inaccessibility as much as joy; there may be almost more pleasure in the recollection than there had been at the event itself. The one from the year before had taken place here, but it was difficult to recognise the location. I could not conceive that the sullen mud could once have been unyielding, with the grass firm and dry above its base. I had helped a child find his parents and, rapturous and lachrymose with joy, they invited me join in their picnic. The little chap had only been missing a quarter of an hour, but the couple treated me as if I had rescued him from a burning building, and insisted I partake of their excellent wine. It was of a Château which I cannot remember, but of such quality that I wondered briefly if the family were aristocratic.

This place, this part of the common, is often in my consciousness. The bending poplar and staid oak peer over my shoulder. It often comes to mind as I tap into the computer at work, and I have never understood the connection, just as I cannot fathom why the tuning of a piano should make me think of the old town in Hastings.

When I returned the postman had been. There was a postcard from Bamburgh, and I recognised Elizabeth's personality in the neat writing style, which scarcely made its indent on the paper. I was astonished to receive it, though I recalled exchanging addresses at the end of the country hike. Perhaps it was by way of apology for the crowded walk; perhaps it was an invitation to a deeper acquaintance; or perhaps she was simply an assiduous correspondent with all her acquaintances.

I saw a carving of an angel on a church so I thought of you. I've had a good time on my half-term break. It was great to catch up with everyone at the night-shelter and help out a little. I've had a few days to myself also; visiting museums in the city and getting out of town for a walk on the Northumberland coast. See you soon, love Elizabeth.

I stood, entranced, holding the item for a while as I re-read it and gently traced my forefinger over the signature; enchanted at receiving such a rare gift. For a moment I imagined being there with her, walking on the bleak sandy beaches of north-east England (though why on earth would one volunteer to do this in late autumn?) but enjoying the drink afterwards, after we shook the sand out of the walking boots and tidied our tousled hair. The sensation disappeared rapidly, and all I had was a card, which I placed on the mantelpiece.

Should I reply? She had included her address as a reminder, so the invitation was clear. But in what manner? A letter might be too formal, and there would be too little to say. A postcard from your home town would appear too eccentric. I settled on a Christmas card; it was not so far off.

During the day I did little but read my biography of Ranji, and drink tea. By mid afternoon I grew restless, and felt that the early winter dusk might be better accompanied by the warmth and cheer of Graham and Jane's house. I was well enough known to them to let myself in by way of the back door, and I stumbled over muddy shoes and wellington boots in the stone-floored porch, smelling the tea, toast and wood smoke from within.

'Brian! How nice!' exclaimed Jane, as she turned to greet me from the stove. 'Emily, put the kettle on and make a pot of tea,' she said to the quiet, long-haired girl who was helping her with the baking. She addressed me again, pushing back strands of her hair from her face with the back of her oven-gloved hand. 'What a lovely surprise!'

'I was just passing,' I explained. 'It's always nice to call by.'

'It's good to see you. Well done on your answer last night! We won!'

'We did indeed.' She could be quite competitive, could Jane.

'Do go on through to the living room and sit down, won't you?' she added. 'I'll be through soon. Emily, take Uncle Brian's coat.'

'Brian hello!' announced Graham immediately. 'Suggestive biscuit?' he asked, proffering the plate. He enjoyed deliberate Malapropisms. 'I wouldn't recommend the others. Desecrated coconut.'

'Yes, Daddy,' said Lorna, sat on the floor by the coffee table. 'Why do we have both yummy biscuits and non-yummy biscuits with dried coconut on them? Why don't we just have yummy ones?'

'Well,' explained Graham. 'That's simple, actually. If they were all yummy, they wouldn't last very long at all, would they?'

'So you choose some things in the supermarket precisely because we *don't* like them?'

'No, no, no. I buy a selection. That way we appreciate them more.'

'No we don't. We just wait for them to go stale and give them to Buster and they make his teeth go bad.'

Graham looked at me more seriously and added, 'Well Brian, what's gone wrong with the cricket? Really, I thought the England batting yesterday was pathetic.'

I guiltily agreed. It was early in the southern hemisphere summer but already the England games, and their defeats, had begun. An unfortunate effect of being a fan is that one becomes personally responsible for the failings of the national team – though never, it seems, for the successes. Another oddity about the observations of the occasional viewers like Graham is their tendency to ascribe failure in the middle order to moral weakness. 'The bowling was pretty good,' I began.

'They just lack backbone. Well, never mind, help me with this.'

Graham was seated in his super hi-tech wheelchair appliance, designed by himself and NASA, or some similar institution, leaning over the low coffee table, which had a chess set laid out. Lorna was looking confident and relaxed.

'I think she's got you cornered,' I announced, with mock gravity.

'England lost,' announced the son, Edward, the youngest of the family.

'At what?' asked Graham. 'Cricket or rugby?'

'Both,' he replied. Graham and I roared with laughter. 'Why are you laughing? It's not funny.'

'It is after 30 years,' said Graham. 'Look at this,' he declared, changing the subject abruptly, waving his well-thumbed copy of *New Scientist* at me. 'Before long we'll be able to use human embryos to grow cells to cure Parkinson's. That's progress, don't you think?'

'Makes me shiver,' I replied sharply. 'Sounds like the Nazis.'

'Come now,' he replied. 'You cannot be against this. It's not human life.'

Jane,who had joined us from the kitchen, cut in. 'Graham, don't be so provoking. Behave.'

'Nonsense, dear. Brian loves to have a debate,' Graham continued, with a cheerful grin on his round bearded face. 'I suppose you object to all kinds of research that takes us out of Edwardian life – you know, devolutionary theory; phonetic engineering.'

'Graham!' Jane yelled. 'Not in front of the children, please.'

Lorna looked up suitably perplexed. 'Phonetic's not a rude word is it Mummy?'

'Well, no, but it's the wrong one. Daddy's being silly.'

'As a matter of fact, your Dad can be very funny,' I offered, intending to show my support. 'He should try stand-up.' I began to raise my hand to my mouth in horror at my appalling gaffe, then realized that the whole family were laughing, so I quickly tried to pass it off as humour.

'Good one, Brian!' said Graham. 'Edgy – I like it. The best comedy is near to the knuckle! Reminds me of when I was a councillor, and a member of the Standing Committee for the Disabled. I kept complaining about the lack of a career ladder for wheelchair-users, but no one ever got the joke.'

'Probably because you were by far the most successful person in the room, at a guess,' I suggested.

Lorna cried out, 'Daddy, it's still your turn!'

After Daddy's rather ingenious move, the girl turned to me. Can you help me, Uncle Brian?

'I think Uncle Brian's a little out of his depth on this one,' I said, drinking up my tea. 'Can't stay, anyway. I have to fly.'

'Oh, stay for a drink. Give me a game of chess,' protested Graham. 'Persuade me that the earth is flat after all.'

'No,' I said, getting up. 'I'll give you a game this evening in the Swan. I said I'd call in on Godfrey and I want to be back for the highlights.'

'Well what's the point in that? We lost, didn't we?'

I furrowed my brow and returned his perplexed look. 'Well, I don't watch for the result.'

'Suit yourself,' he said cheerily. 'See you later.'

'Yes, bye. Bye, Emily! Bye Edward! Bye Lorna!'

Jane saw me out after the children had bid their goodbyes. 'Sorry you couldn't stay long,' she said, with her customary cheery smile. 'You must come back soon.'

'I look forward to that. Cheerio.'

Back out on the street it was now quite dark and even colder. I wondered why I had told a lie about needing to see the vicar, and why my desire to join the warm convivial household of Graham and Jane had been matched by an equally strong impulse to escape so shortly after. I went back home, shivered, and lit a fire. I picked up my book, and began to read. I did not watch the highlights. Of course, only a few moments' contemplation provided the answer. It was not in Graham's gentle satire of my conservative views on science and religion, nor in the banter about the England cricket team's batting performance, nor in my aversion to challenging his superior powers on the chessboard. It was their Russian doll. Their beautiful, Russian doll, and my shame at my envy.

9

End of year rewards

The King's Head was at one end of the high street, and was generally considered a less agreeable pub than The Swan, with its excellent fine ale and cosy snug. It was, however, large, and with an extension, and so popular for functions. The single-storey appendage to an otherwise elderly building had been designed by a myopic architect ignorant of the risks of rising damp and invasive mould. It even had a corrugated roof. I had volunteered to track down the planning officer who had given approval some 20 years earlier, but learnt that he had left the country. In any case, the others said that they liked it. As I arrived for the annual awards dinner, most of the players and some of their partners had arrived and were seated at a long table set up for the event. It was early December, and the event doubled as a Christmas party for the cricketers and their families, the one major get-together in the long wintry close season in these northern latitudes.

There was a sports' fan's avid discussion already in full flow: who would you pick in your all-time best cricket eleven?

No two fans will produce the same list. Quite promptly they asked me.

'Jack Hobbs and Gordon Greenidge to open,' I began. Murmurs of approval. 'Like it,' said Tony. 'Old and new; orthodoxy and flair.'

'Of course, you saw Jack Hobbs play, didn't you?' quipped Eric.

'Cheeky,' I replied. 'Though I think he was still alive when I was born.' I continued: 'Sir Don at three; Sachin Tendulkar at four.'

'Bold choice!' said Craig McAllister, our quick bowler from Leith, who remarkably never protested at the stultifyingly unoriginal nickname 'Jock' – indeed, rather took pride in it. 'He's still young. You think he's the real deal?'

'Absolutely,' I said. 'Probably the best batsman I've seen. Brian Lara's worth a mention, too. So, Graeme Pollock at five, Sir Gary at six. Alan Knott seven, Kapil Dev eight, Malcolm Marshall, Wes Hall and Jim Laker. Maybe Faroukh Engineer as keeper.

Craig reminisced ... 'Kapil Dev! Best bit of cricket in Test Match history. Bodger and I were at Lords in 1990 ...'

'I know what you're going to say...' I chipped in.

'India needed 24 to avoid the follow-on when the ninth wicket fell,' said Craig with enthusiasm. 'He didn't rate the number 11 so he hit four sixes in consecutive balls off Eddie Hemmings. Pure class. Pure fucking class. All the England fans were cheering.'

We all beamed at the memory. I had only seen the highlights on TV.

'Keano, your turn,' said Craig.

'Easy,' he said. 'Picks itself. To open: Herbert Sutcliffe and Sir Len.'

Everyone groaned. 'This is supposed to be the best world team, not the best Yorkshire team,' said Eric.

Dave appeared pleased and unapologetic. 'There's not much difference, I grant thee. Herbert Sutcliffe is the only England batsman to average over 60. Len Hutton averaged over 50 despite a war injury.'

'He's got a point on the openers,' I said.

Reassured by my nod of approval, the others continued to listen, though Tony piped up: 'Maybe it would be easier just to ask him which non-Yorkshire players he picked.'

'Well, four made the grade,' explained David. 'Sir Don, Sir Gary, Malcolm Marshall and Dennis Lillee – honorary Yorkshireman.'

'Who have you got keeping wicket, then?'

'Jimmy Binks.'

'Jimmy who?' said Craig.

'Jimmy Binks.'

'He never even played for England!' protested Tony.

'Actually,' I said. 'He played twice against India in the '63-64 tour. Scored a half-century I think.'

'Hardly makes him one of the best of all time,' said Tony. 'What about Rod Marsh or Godfrey Evans or Wasim Bari?' This was in the days before Adam Gilchrist rendered debates on 'greatest wicketkeeper-batsman of all time' more or less redundant.

'My Dad and his brothers reckon he had the best glove-work of any, and he was a tough, nuggety batsman. Difficult to get out. You'd want him on your side.'

'OK. So,' said Craig: 'What about your spin bowler?'

'Hedley Verity,' replied Dave. 'It was between him and Jim Laker, who played for Surrey but hailed from Yorkshire.'

'Hedley Verity was a great bowler and a war hero,' I said.

'Match-winner in the Lords Ashes test in 1934 and killed in the Italian campaign. His last words were: "Keep going lads".' Dave's eyes misted over and so did mine.

'They don't make them like that any more,' he said. 'We must never forget his contribution to Yorkshire cricket, England cricket and peace and democracy in western Europe.'

'That's just about the order of priorities in Keano's world, ain't it?' observed Eric. 'But if Yorkshire's so great,' he asked him. 'What are you doing living down here then?'

'Diplomatic posting,' said Keano, with an impeccably straight face. The real reason was a promising marketing post at the European headquarters of a multinational company near Portsmouth. Quite how he felt engaged with promoting any product or service that did not pertain to the holy land of Yorkshire was a mystery to us all. His favourite trivia quiz question was: 'Only three English clubs have won t' First Division three seasons in a row: Arsenal, Liverpool and which other?' At this point he would point to the Huddersfield Town replica football shirt he habitually wore, too impatient for anyone to guess the answer.

Eric looked at me. 'I've never actually been to Yorkshire. Are they all like that there?'

'Well, they love their cricket,' I said, a closet Yorkshire-admirer. 'Fancy a pint?'

'Yea, cheers Col.'

In the queue for drinks at the bar I was behind Julie, Eric's very attractive and very organised young wife, and her close friend Nisha, who had begun dating Craig McAllister. Such is the proximity in such situations that one could not help but overhear the conversation, and it was quickly evident, even without his name being uttered, that the subject matter was Eric.

'I mean, in the summer I'm a cricket widow; in the winter I'm used to being a football widow. He's cutting down on that but taking up golf! I mean, if was a real widow at least I'd get the life insurance.'

Nisha whistled and giggled nervously. 'Ouch! Let's hope he doesn't suffer an accident – you'd be getting your collar felt!'

'Well really. I mean, I don't mind having time to myself and my friends, it's more Jack I'm concerned about 'cos he wants his Dad around. I mean, I kick the ball to Jack in the park, but it's not the same. It's really frustrating because Eric's actually a good Dad with the kids, when he's around.'

'Well, you've got that at least.'

'Yes, at least.'

They gathered their white wine spritzers and returned to the table.

After I was served I gathered the pints in my hands, the two cold glasses pressed against each for support as I manoeuvred my way between the closely gathered throng. I just managed to avoid bumping into Carole, wife of the captain Derek, as she waited in the queue behind me.

'Good evening, Carole,' I said, with, for no particular reason, an exaggerated flourish.

'What a gentleman you are, Brian,' she replied, her face broadening into a rare smile. 'How nice to be addressed "good evening" and not "hiya" or "oi".'

I smiled. 'Or even just a grunt.'

'Youth today!' she said. 'You weren't like that when you were young, were you, Brian?'

'I'm not sure I ever was young,' I replied.

'Of course,' she said, but gave me a concerned look. 'You were brought up as a gentleman. It's nothing to be ashamed of. You're probably the last one left.'

'Oh, I don't know,' I said. 'There's Derek…'

She raised her gaze upwards with disdain. 'Don't spoil your manners with sarcasm, please Brian. Look at him,' she added, turning round to offer a tired gaze in Derek's direction. He was waiting for his drink in the bar rather than in the dining area, thirsty and impatient for his first pint. 'He'll soon be quaffing a pint of beer and wiping his 'tache with the reverse of his sleeve. Please don't tell me he's some kind of Roger Moore.'

'Well, he's honest,' I said. 'And works very hard as club captain.'

I returned to the table. Nisha and Julie were sat next to each other, facing Craig and Eric; the four of them immediately to my left. Tony and David Keane, having slid down to join us for the important debate on who really should feature in the greatest Test Match XI of all time – a matter sadly still unresolved to this day, with the exception of the position of wicketkeeper – had rejoined a group at the farther end of the long table.

'We blokes do sometimes envy women and gay men,' said Craig. He loved to be provocative, and I could tell from the swagger in his voice that he was pitching for an argument across the gender divide. 'I mean, you get such pleasure from simple things, like having a coffee or shopping. We have to pull a gorgeous bird or score a fifty or something. It's much more effort.'

'And do we get the recognition?' asked Eric, presumably rhetorically.

'I hope you haven't been "pulling gorgeous birds"!' Julie quipped.

'Well, you're gorgeous darling,' he said. 'Of course, in my day…'

'Your "days" are behind you, I can tell you that for nothing,' she said.

'It's a load of rubbish, what you've just said, of course,' said Nisha. 'What about drinking beer and watching football on the telly? That hardly requires any effort.'

'Well, fair point,' said Eric. 'Though watching England can be hard work. Could be worse though, could be Scotland!' he nudged Craig in the ribs. The two were good friends. Just then the waitress appeared at the table to take orders. She was comely, with a cute blond bob, and flashed a little cleavage. Most male heads turned around.

'Look at them!' exclaimed Nisha. 'So shallow! You see, that's the real difference between men and women. You go for superficial looks. We're attracted by character and sense of humour.'

'What a load of rubbish,' said Eric. 'Biggest load of bollocks I heard in my entire life. What about when you two are watching the Wimbledon, drooling over Andre Agassi changing his shirt? Are you really thinking: "Hmm great sense of humour!" Load of bollocks. Why don't you fancy Groucho Marx or Danny de Vito instead?'

Nisha had the decency to blush a little. 'Weeell,' she said. 'I think Andre Agassi does have a great sense of humour.' But she effectively conceded, making the point in a self-mocking tone of voice.

'I think his arms, shoulders and bearing strongly indicate a great character,' said Julie, sending herself up with a saucy voice. 'His thighs too.' The four of them laughed.

Craig said, provocatively: 'Some women do fancy Danny de Vito.'

'You're kidding?' replied Eric. 'That's not deep – that's just weird.'

For the dinner, Hector and I, the two single gentlemen, were sat opposite each other. To my right was Carole, and facing her was Derek. The seat arrangers tended to assume that this trio would be the most natural company for me, with Hector being introverted and serious, and Carole and Derek closer to me in age. In fact, I was more drawn to the more vibrant chat of the two younger couples to my left, but wasn't always able to become part of their repartee, so closely knit were they.

'Bloody good do, again,' said Derek to me, after I had let the handsome quartet to my left converse among themselves. 'Good food.'

I munched heartlessly on a leathery piece of chicken and some cold slices of carrot.

He tried again. 'Good season, wasn't it? Some bloody good wins. Away at Chiddingfold!' He still had a pint of beer on the go, its white froth sliding reluctantly down the glass, next to a short beaker of cheap wine.

'It seems a long time ago,' I said.

'I like having the do at this time, though,' said Derek. 'Becomes like a Christmas event. Where are you going to put the trophy this year? Going for a change of room?'

This departure from his customary envy was admirable, and deserved a generous response, which I failed to muster. 'No, the mantelpiece, I think. I might be moving home, though.'

'What? That would be something. You've lived there all your life, haven't you?'

'Not quite.'

'You'd be staying round here, though?' he asked, sounding genuinely anxious.

'Oh, yes.' I said.

He drained his glass. ''Ere, Carole, could you get me another beer?'

'You've hardly finished the last one,' she said with a disapproving scowl. 'You shouldn't be mixing beer and wine.' She moved his wine glass away from his elbow, in the manner of someone performing a routine task.

The conversation for the rest of the meal was unremarkable. After the dessert Derek tapped a spoon against a glass, got himself to his feet and walked down to the end of the room, next to a side table on which were placed the array of trophies to be awarded. 'Can I have your attention, please! Hello? Good. It has fallen to me, as the one in the club with the biggest gob and the worst record – and therefore least likely to have picked up any gongs – to make the speech for this season's awards.' There was loud applause.

'We have had an auspicious season once again – try me in half an hour and I won't be able to say auspicious – noted for my heroic innings of 10 not out lasting 40 minutes at Coldharbour, joining the league and not getting relegated, an epic tour to Somerset and the invasion of cows at Findon.

'First we have the award for batsman of the year, which goes, as it always does, to Mr B Clarke, better known as Col. Nine hundred and thirty-two runs at an average of 55. Only two centuries this year, mind, you're slipping. Before I give the award, can I just make one simple request. Col: why don't we just come over to your place next year, save us the bother of moving this heavy old cup out of its place every time?'

'Suits me!' I called out.

'That way we can finally get at your Scotch,' he added.

'If you can find the key!' I called out, before walking up to receive the trophy. I wanted to announce: 'I don't like winning. I don't like being marked out as different. I am tired of being unique', but I did not. Instead I shuffled up to the top table, picked up the cup, let it fall with its familiar weight as I held on with one hand, and returned.

'And now to the bowler of the year, going, for the first time, to a bowler with the weirdest action and the weirdest name. Ladies and gentleman, the nicest fella in the club, Kennel 'imself– otherwise known as Hector Sprake!'

A bemused Hector made his procession, red in the face, like an apprentice on a hoax errand.

At the end of the ceremonies, Derek proposed a toast to his wife Carole. 'You know, I said to her just the other evening: "We've been married for 15 years. Do you think we'll ever have sex again?" and she replies: "I dunno. There's no one I really fancy at the moment – do *you* have someone in mind?"!'

The lads roared with laughter, and I did too, though I worried slightly the dialogue may have been genuine. I took a comfort break and nipped out to the gentleman's. On my way back, weaving my way through a crowded public bar, the hubbub building, I was astonished to see Elizabeth, in a posh black velvety evening frock, silvery necklace in place, walking away from the bar with, I could detect, a glass in each hand; one of wine, and a half-pint of beer. The sight of two vessels filled me immediately with a sensation of jealousy and grief that hurt. Though it pained me to do so, I followed her progress as she delicately sought to keep the glasses upright while picking a route carefully among the throng. Her course was principally from left to right as I watched and I thought I was hidden from her view. But a movement of people to her left as someone rose from a table caused her to change direction, and she spotted me.

'Colin, how nice to see you!' It was a warmer greeting than I would have expected.

'It's nice to see you too,' I said with relief, but somewhat warily. I paused as we made brief eye contact. 'Perhaps I shouldn't keep you from your … friend.' I added, nodding briefly at the two glasses.

'Oh, no, they can wait,' she said casually. 'I'm just here with my hiking buddies for a Christmas get-together. This is a half a shandy for my friend Jenny. The walkers usually have a seasonal do, I've learned. I didn't realize we'd be clashing with the cricket club! But I'm glad I bumped into you – almost literally, as it turned out. When I found out the cricketers were here I thought I would come over and say hello - I've only just got here. It's crowded, isn't it?'

'Yes, but I guess most evenings are, this time of year. You'd always be clashing with someone, though maybe not such heavy drinkers as cricketers!'

She laughed. 'It's four-deep at the bar!'

'Thanks for the postcard – nice surprise! You should have received my Christmas card.'

'Yes, thanks!' she replied.

We were raising our voices above the din. I paused as I wondered: might I propose another meeting? A date – a real one, this time, without a sect of the Socialist Workers Party on its rural retreat keeping us company? My hesitation was not caused by mere reserve or shyness, but an altogether more fierce emotion: the fear of rejection. My few recent – and by recent, I refer to previous years, not months – attempts to inquire of a single lady if she would like to join me for an evening meal or even a coffee had been rather brusquely dismissed, often in a manner that reflected disdain, rather than mere lack of interest. The manner of The Rebuff in social language seemed to have become more cold and matter-of-fact with the passing of the years. I could not help but reach the conclusion that it was another baleful consequence of the informality and casual indifference of our modern culture. Since the Swinging Sixties made promiscuity so fashionable, with sex viewed as no more than a recreation, The Rebuff has become as much a part of the modern woman's array of accessories as her handbag, and even more necessary, given the heightened expectation by many men that sex can come without obligation. The Rebuff is, of course, and of necessity, I accept, delivered with the same practised coldness and minimum of eye contact, in the few cases where an interest is sincere as in the majority where it is not; but the emotional impact on the male suitor whose intentions are honourable are as great – or of course, probably rather greater – than those with a more selfish, opportunistic impulse.

So instead I said simply: 'Well – it's nice to see you. And Happy Christmas.'

'Happy Christmas!' she replied, more joyously than I, with a wide smile. She leaned forward and pecked me lightly on the cheek, once. I inhaled a delicate hint of fragrance, and the exotic scent caused an invasion of nostalgia and desire in me such as that from another era or even another life.

'Let's stay in touch,' I said.

'Yes, let's meet in the New Year,' she replied.

I returned to the table, a touch more cheerful and with a spring in my step.

'Who is that lovely-looking lady you were chatting with just there Col?' asked Eric, in a teasing but friendly manner. He had just returned from the bar and had witnessed the chat.

'Oh, Elizabeth. I know her from church,' I said, trying to sound off-hand.

'So are you, you know, dating?'

'What?' I said. 'Don't be ridiculous.' I felt warm and was probably blushing.

'What's ridiculous about that? Is she already married?'

'Well, no, as it happens.'

'Well, you should ask her out, then.'

'What? No way.'

'Why? What's wrong with her?'

'What's *wrong* with Elizabeth? Oh, just about everything! Where do I even begin? She's kind, cultured, incredibly intelligent, great sense of humour, mature, well read and caring, with a lovely nature. Plus she's attractive. Way out of my league.' I took a long swig of the fresh pint of beer he had kindly bought for me. 'I wouldn't go out with someone who would go out with me. No – much safer to live alone.'

'Just as well you're not as defeatist as that when it comes to cricket. You'd never play an attacking shot,' said Eric.

'Yes, well, in cricket there are rules.'

10

The long cold spring

For all my solitary status, I looked forward to Christmas, especially the day itself. The morning service was always joyous and, most years, I was very generously invited to have Christmas dinner with Graham, Jane and their lovely children. They treated me as a family member. I stayed for lunch and for afternoon board games, offered generous gifts to the children; and I always took care to depart in the early evening before becoming a burden. With this combination of cheery company and solitude, the evening was a time for peace and reflection, not loneliness or melancholy.

In the bitter late winter, I saw Elizabeth from time to time, on the occasion that she attended at All Saints. She greeted me as we passed in the aisle or porch, and sometimes we chatted briefly about the service or the weather; at all times friendly but a touch reserved. She had said at the awards event 'Let's see each other in the New Year', which naturally was a phrase that echoed in my head in the short cold days of late winter and early spring. Did she really mean it? Is this what she meant

– the occasional polite greeting by a gravestone in the All Saints churchyard – or should I take the initiative to propose a meeting? Was she regretting having made this suggestion, or feeling mildly snubbed that I had not taken the initiative to respond with an invitation?

On a few occasions, I came close to calling. I had been in possession of her telephone number since the time of the walk in the autumn, and I wrote it out on a pad by the phone, on the well-polished tiny upright table in the hall, often alongside some handwritten notes-to-self as to how I might begin a conversation, for example: 'Ah, Elizabeth, it's Brian Clarke here…' Or: 'Good evening – remember me? We bumped into each other at the Christmas do in the King's Head and you suggested we meet up in the New Year …'

Sometimes my trembling left index finger completed digit four or even five of the six-numbered code but then abandoned the enterprise, with a fear of sounding stilted and rehearsed if I followed the scrawled autocue, or mumbling and incoherent if I did not. Then there was the uncertainty over whether to introduce myself Brian – my real name, but one she seemed reluctant to deploy and may not recognize – or Colin. Amid the multitude of conflicting suggestions in my head, and without a confidant to guide me, I erred on the side of hesitation, doubt, introversion and self-pity – a combination, I reflected, that had reliably protected me from heartbreak in the past.

Spring finally came. There was a newcomer to the team. I greeted Dale cheerily as I met him on a bright but cold April evening for a net practice, but the dark-haired giant was inexpressive in reply.

'He's a fast bowler,' explained Derek. 'We need one. Keano's gone back to Yorkshire, did you hear?'

I had. David Keane had met some of us in the pub a month or so earlier. 'I've got a dream posting,' he explained. 'Assistant press officer Yorkshire Dales Tourist Board. Chance like that might only come round once in a lifetime. Plan on playing for Burley-in-Wharfedale – proper Yorkshire League cricket. Imagine!' His eyes misted over with emotion. We looked on enviously.

I wouldn't have told Hurricane, but if anything the new youngster Dale was a touch quicker. It meant that I enjoyed the practice more. I loved the quicks, and the ball comes quicker still off the smooth plastic surface we used for practice. I batted first, glad to wear the pads and gloves against the chill; exhilarated by the depth to which the fresh breeze reached into my lungs.

Dale was first. It was rapid, but a little astray and too full in pitch. I bent the left knee. Smack! The ball departed sweetly and painlessly from the middle and the net billowed expansively as it absorbed the force. I almost surprised myself at such perfect timing so early in the season. I picked it up from the netting and threw it accurately at the bowler. He tugged it from the air without effort or acknowledgement. His next was fired in short, directed at my eyes. It 'followed' me a little, came on even faster than I expected and I had to lean back sharply to avoid contact. Nice.

'Good bouncer,' I said brightly, returning the ball. There was no reply. He charged in again, fired the ball this time at my body and I fended it off. It flew into the net. Again I threw it back and received an icy glare.

'Where did you find him, then, Derek?' I asked once we were in the pavilion bar afterwards.

'He's just moved into the village. Used to play for Guildford. Worked abroad for a few years,' Derek replied. 'Good, isn't he?'

'Yea, but a miserable so and so. Can't you get him to cheer up?'

'Wouldn't want to!' Derek cackled. 'We need to intimidate the opposition sometimes. Feed him some raw meat!'

Dale had either come with a pre-packaged nickname, or quickly acquired one: Tyson. It was possibly a reference to Frank Tyson, the ultra-fast Northamptonshire and England bowler of the 1950s, but many of the lads were too young to remember him. The origin more probably stemmed from a rumour that he had decked a Frenchman in a bar while working on the vineyards a year or two earlier. Apparently the unlucky Gallic fellow had argued that football had not really been invented in England. As the rumour first circulated in the dressing room, there were murmurs of approval and a sentiment of 'Well, fair enough'. I looked over at where the dark-haired giant leaned over the snooker table, sank the ball, then missed one and retired for his pint.

I looked out of the window and was alarmed to see Bodger apparently struggling with a dreadful injury, his left knee stuck awkwardly outwards as he stumbled slowly with a heavy limp. Only as he resumed a normal gait and continued crossing the gravelly car park did I realise he had been stubbing out a cigarette. He whistled and grinned as he skipped up the few steps and entered. He had missed practice but called in for a drink. As he offered the newcomer Dale a fresh pint, I looked with copious envy for signs that Dale treated him with even less respect than he did me, being alternately dismayed by a shared communication and cheered by an indifferent stare.

The evening was drawing in, and I headed home. The air was still light but even chillier, with a shower threatening. On the edge of the Common, I spied a familiar figure, hunched once again over what may have been a map or a leaflet. I approached with confidence.

For many men, emotion or desire are insufficient spurs for decisiveness: we need an activity. Having declined, for a full four months, to call Elizabeth, lacking a pretext for a call and presuming desire for my company to be insufficient attraction, I divined an opportunity to be her guide, given my long-established local knowledge of the terrain.

'Lost again?' I asked. 'You're on the Common.'

As Elizabeth looked up, I sensed that much would depend on her expression as our eyes met: whether excited, engaged, friendly, lukewarm, indifferent, or irritated. There was a spectrum. Our eyes met. Definitely towards the left-hand end. A warm surge of relief flowed through my body.

'I know perfectly well where I am. I've just completed a walk and have begun plotting the next. Time for a drink. You joining me, Colin?'

Easy as that.

'Yes, lovely!' I said. I then scolded myself. '"Lovely?" What heterosexual man says "Lovely" these days? Where did *that* word come from?' Yet she did not seem to mind either the content or manner of my reply, and briskly walked alongside me, with a natural ease.

The shower suddenly escalated into a torrent. I observed: 'This seems to be a habit of ours, getting stuck on the edge of a Common in the rain.'

She put up her hood. 'You haven't any jacket at all, just that cricket sweater!' she exclaimed. 'You'll be soaked through! Shall we go into that pub there?'

'Oh not the Star! It's really rather rough for someone like you. Can't we go on to The Swan down the road?'

'What do you mean, "For someone like me?",' she said,

sounding simultaneously full of mirthful curiosity and mild offence. I felt mortified. I meant: a smoky joint full of beery bikers with pool cues was not a place for an educated lady, but I said nothing.

She continued: 'I've been a social worker. I've taught in schools with an intake so rough the police arrive in groups. I've helped build latrines in some of the poorest places in the world, where you can hear the shell-fire in the distance, and where the locals celebrate feasts by firing live rounds into the air. I think I can handle a pub in mid-Sussex with the smell of smoke and a few stains on the floor.'

'Well, you've been warned,' I began.

'How far is The Swan?'

'Another hundred yards or so.'

'That's far too far. We'll just step in here while the shower passes over.'

'Oh, um, OK.'

My spirits sank as I saw the crowd of regulars smoking near the bar and the menacing-looking youths with their ragged tee-shirts at the pool table in the public bar, through a doorway in the back of the saloon, which was where we entered. A couple of large individuals with massive tattoos and biker jackets slouched by the wall, smoking. Elizabeth, by contrast, seemed quite cheerful.

'At least there's a table near the window in the saloon bar,' I said. 'What'll you have?'

'Orange juice, please.'

'A pint of best and an orange juice, please,' I said with as much confidence as I could muster as I reached the bar. To my surprise the proprietor was youthful and smartly dressed, and the place seemed efficiently run, but he glowered at my very presence as he took the order, the pale blue eyes scowling behind the fringe of brown hair.

We occupied the table near the window. I felt both relieved and anxious. We asked each other how our winter had been, but had scarcely begun the conversation when the landlord entered from the public bar, paused for a while and looked moodily at us, annoyed, perhaps, that we had not yet finished our drinks. He could find no one else in the saloon bar, in spite of his raking the place with a stare and pottering over to the far corner to convince himself, so he returned through the door. Then he reappeared immediately and interrupted us directly. 'Come on, could you be moving out of the saloon bar, now please? We have a function on,' he ordered. 'Can't you see the sign? Can you read?'

He pointed to a drooping card, held in a metal stand, that bore the legend 'Private Function'. It stood a little way to the right of the entrance area; a different angle from the route to the bar.

'I didn't notice it, no,' I replied. 'I think we'd rather stay here if that's all right – you've only just served us, and we've only just sat down,' I protested, wincing at the thought of taking Elizabeth into the dingy public bar with its crude men and pool table.

'Well I'm sorry but you can't stay here. You can move to the public bar if you like.'

I thought of the dreadful youths in the public bar. 'Well it seems hardly reasonable...' I began.

Elizabeth charitably offered: 'Come on, Colin, we might as well go to the bar – we could even have a game of pool!' she added with a nervous chuckle, sounding semi-serious.

'But I don't want to,' I said, stubbornly.

The landlord was unyielding. 'I am the proprietor, and I want this room for a private function; to which you are not invited. Understand?' His voice had grown menacing.

'All I was saying was that we've only just sat down and you've only just served us. So I'm bound to ask why if you start moving us around...' I explained.

'Look, just get out will you, you ponce?' he exploded suddenly, his bulbous, tanned face screwed up with disdain, his grey eyes brimming with bile. 'I've had enough of people like you. Just fuck off, will you?'

'How dare you use language like that!' I began. 'OK we'll go into the public bar.'

'No. Tell you what,' he said. 'Don't stop there, just get out will you?'

'You don't have to encourage us,' I said as we moved to the door. 'I would never set foot in this place again!'

'Well you wouldn't be allowed, anyway. You're barred!' he yelled.

We stood on the pavement in the rain, momentarily too upset for words. 'I'm most terribly sorry,' I explained after a while. 'I have never been spoken to like that before in more than 40 years living here!'

'That's quite all right: it wasn't your fault,' she replied. 'And you did warn me.' She was actually rather amused, while I was trembling with indignation.

'Listen,' I said. 'Why don't we have a drink some other time, in dry clothes, at a civilized venue, from which we are not excluded on the grounds of unreasonable behaviour, mild offence or inverted snobbery?' I took myself by surprise with such self-confidence. It is remarkable what a little anger can do.

To my delight and quiet surprise, she replied: 'I would love that – assuming of course you plan on continuing to behave reasonably.'

I smiled briskly. 'Well, can I just point out that I've never been barred from a pub before I met you?'

She smiled at that. 'Fair point!'

I continued: 'But to put your mind at rest, I shall cancel all plans for supermarket trolley-racing, traffic cone theft and skinny dipping in public fountains immediately.'

'Splendid,' she said.

11

Clumsy angel

I spent a long time deciding what to wear and how to present myself. A tie? Or no tie? A suit would be absurdly formal, I reflected – I'm meeting a sophisticated lady for a drink, not representing an individual in court – but at least a jacket of some sort? I don't 'do' casual attire, and it would not suit me in any case. Yes, that would be the right balance. Smart trousers, best blazer, shirt with a collar but no tie. I looked in the mirror. Something felt wrong; the shirt without a tie just seemed too artfully casual and possibly pretentious, reminding me of the manner in which young men at a formal awards event, towards the end of an evening, draped their disentangled bow ties casually around their neck, largely to demonstrate that it was the genuine article and that such sophisticated souls had mastered the art of its construction. Also, the collar just splayed itself out a bit too far and over the top of the jacket lapel. I selected a tie with informal colours, that seemed to complement the navy blue of the jacket. That's better.

Then I located my best shoes, which turned out to be scuffed and grubby. Not daring to take the risk of black polish becoming smeared on trousers and jacket, I partially undressed before buffing up the footwear, then got dressed again, and shod, and checked again in the mirror. A bit too formal, I thought, but better than trying to be Mick Jagger.

We had a mid-evening rendezvous, each having eaten at home, and I offered to collect her from her home address before we drove to a country pub that I recommended. I found her home from the address easily enough, but once parked outside, began to feel restless and uncomfortable again. How could I feel more nervous before a social engagement with a perfectly friendly and engaging soul, than I would feel when addressing the court on behalf of a client, or opening the batting against a fast bowler on a sporting pitch in April? What's the worst thing that could happen? I reflected. Unfortunately, I then began to think of several worst things, each perfectly plausible, such as: a clumsy faux pas, an accidental insult to Elizabeth's world view, a general air of pomposity and conservatism, resulting in her disinclination to meet again, leading to my renewed loneliness and bachelor status, increasing alcohol dependency, physical and mental decline and premature death with only a handful of the lads from the cricket club attending the funeral, and even those largely due to the promise of free drinks paid out of my estate; Godfrey mustering some positive attributes from long-ago anecdotes as he attempts to muster an emotional eulogy; people shuffling uncomfortably in the cold and nearly-empty church, a neat row of Batting Awards lined atop the coffin, representing the only tangible achievements of a once promising but ultimately futile existence.

So, yes, there was plenty to be nervous about. Plus, this tie makes me look too formal, I thought suddenly. I ripped it off, stepped out of the car and approached the door, knocking sharply with the metal ring. There was no bell.

'Oh,' I said, as the door yielded and revealed a teenage girl in casual clothes, who looked at me with pity and amusement.

'I'm sorry,' I said hurriedly. 'I must have the wrong address.' I turned to go.

'Are you Colin?' she asked suddenly.

'Er, yes.'

'Mum's expecting you.'

Mum? I tried to avoid an expression of shock, though probably unnecessarily given that the girl had turned smartly away and was scampering into the front room to find Elizabeth.

Mum. Was this the reason for the departure from the convent? Had there been a terrible scandal? Why would such a sensitive person appear to bear no scars? Why had she not told me? This girl is nearly 20. It must have happened years ago!

Mum. I had always felt distanced from the term. Aunty Kath was always Aunty Kath, never 'Mum'. I would sometimes be jealous of school friends, but they were more jealous of me; of the roomy freedom in the old house, the conservatory with old cricket bags, the feast of toys in the chest, the perennial smell of bakewell tart. All this without a Mum. My parents had died when I was only eight, killed in aircraft accident on their way home from a skiing holiday. My Aunt Kath had brought me up. It was good of her, really, given that I always had an air of guilt over the fate of her late husband.

I was only six or seven, waiting in my parents' car, while they chatted with Aunty Kath in the sitting room. I was playing with a functionless strap sown into the grey leather rear seat. It grew warm and I felt both sticky and rather bored. I began to open the door and then shut it suddenly, enjoying the slam! as it closed. Then I did the opposite; closing slowly but opening suddenly, enjoying the mechanics of the exercise, as all small boys do, until at one point I felt a contact with a moving vehicle. I only remember specific mute images. Memory records not in moving pictures but in still life. I remember Uncle Gerald, as he lay on the tarmac, blood seeping from a wound, perhaps from an elbow or his head; the black, stately bicycle to which his legs still clung as the front wheel continued to whir; the grey, upholstered inside of the car door as I lowered my gaze below window level; and then Aunty Kath looking down at me in fear and concern. He was concussed and suffered wounds and, it seemed to me, never quite the same after. He died about a year later and, although the grown-ups were keen to avoid any association with the accident, and indeed he was considerably older than Aunt Kath, a vague sense of responsibility still clung to me. Aunty Kath bore the loss with grace and, if it doesn't sound indelicate, just the merest hint of relief. Uncle Gerald was a fairly severe soul. He didn't suffer fools, but had little time for wise folk either. He had provided for her; shortly after his death she got an office job and did well. We had the inheritance of two good properties plus her salary, so we were never hard-up.

It was only a few months after Uncle Gerald's passing that that my parents were killed. So it was just Aunty Kath and me, with our big house, our love of cricket and *Jennings* books, and the garden and the woods to play in. What a team we made!

In the hall of Elizabeth's maisonette I felt moved by the sparseness, the cheapness of the furnishings, and the worn thin grey carpet. A Christ figure looked out from a picture frame.

'Mum, Colin's here!' the youngster announced as I followed her into the living room. Elizabeth, reclined on the sofa, hands behind her head as though posing for a painting, looked up from her magazine and peered over half-moon glasses. She appeared to enjoy my moment of discomfort as she rose.

'OK, Shelley,' she said to the girl. 'We'll be off now. Are you going to be OK?'

'Yea, sure.' The daughter sat in a sagging bean bag, picked up the remote control and began flicking through the channels.

'Errrm,' I began as we sat in the car.

'I do owe you an explanation,' she said, smiling. 'I'm a foster parent.'

'Can you just leave her for the evening?'

'She's 17; technically not my foster child anymore, but she's been renting this rather poky room in a hostel in Brighton since she left the children's home last year. I let her stay the weekend sometimes when I'm not fostering someone else.'

'Is she ever any trouble?'

'Only to herself,' said Elizabeth, becoming a little sombre for the first time.

'Do you mind that she calls you "mum"?'

'It's the best service I can provide.'

'Do you have to instil discipline? It must be terribly difficult.'

'To begin with I made the opposite mistake. You can forget that they need a huge amount of love and reassurance.'

'I don't know how you can do it. Isn't it hard, just getting to know them and then they go?'

'Sometimes.'

'Are they grateful?' I asked.

'Not verbally,' she conceded, and stayed silent with such determination that I knew not to interrupt.

I drove her to the pub. I had thought about inviting her for dinner, but I recalled an older lady, a friend of Aunt Kath, once advising me as a young man not to be too forward when courting: 'Dinner means bed,' she advised. 'Don't put her off by proposing a candle-lit dinner at the first date or second or third.'

I asked as we sat down: 'How do you spend time with Shelley, now she's no longer little and presumably has her own gang?'

'Well, she's embarrassed to see me on the street when she's with her friends, naturally, but that's perfectly normal and to be expected. She's not without her problems, but she's remarkably sweet-natured, given all she's gone through. Her birth parents were shockingly neglectful but not deliberately cruel. And we have a shared interest: we love to see fantasy movies, and I even encouraged her to start on the Narnia books, though she thinks she's too old for them now, of course. It was nice for me, to go back and re-read *The Lion, The Witch & The Wardrobe* and the others, and just become lost and enraptured again.'

'I have to say I struggled to get into those as a child, though obviously I was aware of them,' I said.

'Didn't you grow up with Tolkein and CS Lewis?'

'No - PG Wodehouse and Anthony Buckeridge.'

'Don't you ever want to escape into a different world?' she asked. 'Explore the contours of a different planet and the imagined customs of an alien species? Or feel the shiver down your spine as a ghost enters the room, noticed by only a few?'

I adored the glint in her eyes as she said these words, and though she half-persuaded me, I felt invited to offer a riposte. Inspired by her grace and intelligence, I began a speech that had formed in my mind over the years, but which I had assumed would never find an audience. 'There is magic in all life; in the every-day,' I replied. 'A spider's web is symmetrical; fragile, yet deadly. A wasp's nest may be a perfect sphere, with parallel internal walls, as though crafted by an expert joiner. Look at your hand. Turn it over. Caress your fingertips with the end of your thumb. Is that not a miracle? Look someone in the eye for a whole minute. These tiny portals, small and sunken. Inwards, they convert light into colour and perspective, to let us see beauty or drama. Outwards, they convey our deepest emotion, the very voice of the soul, to someone else. Is that not a miracle? Why invent other creatures when we do not understand ourselves? Not take the time to appreciate this clumsy angel; divine beast, a human being? We are intensely conscious in almost everything, yet did not choose to exist! We are already supernatural. Composers can communicate across the generations; we can listen to the heaven's width in the timing, in the space, between the notes in a cadence by Scarlatti or Mozart. I get called old-fashioned because I recoil from pop music and from Hollywood blockbusters with their ghouls and super-heroes, and I seek peace and quiet from time to time. Give myself the opportunity to appreciate this unmeasurable force that makes life life. In our modern world one has to plead for permission to slow down, away from the relentless din of popular entertainment, or the noisy hate campaigns between rival politicians. With all progress there is loss, and often the progress is meagre and the loss, immense.'

I paused. My emotional speech at an end, she did look me in the eye, for a long and intense while, with a warmth that felt like, if not love, then the sweetest feeling I had experienced in many years. A lady on the next table, not elderly but a little older than us, whose companion had gone to the bar, gave me a noiseless little round of applause and mouthed the phrase: 'Well said,' with a little appreciative tilt of the head, but then apologized for intruding, being English and all that.

Elizabeth reached forward to tidy the collar on my left-hand side with deft and gentle movements. 'Clumsy angel,' she said to me, tenderly. The collar must have splayed itself outwards after I had removed my tie in the car, and remained at an increasingly ungainly angle throughout our conversation and my little speech. I might have felt patronized but instead I felt moved. Her fingers did not make contact with my skin directly, yet she *touched* me. Then she asked: 'So do you achieve these escapes; find your refuge from our high-decibel culture?'

'Well yes, but rather too much,' I reflected, worrying that I sounded sorry for myself. 'That's the problem.'

12

A domestic

It was May and then it was June. The days lengthened and the weather was fine, for the most part. I was in a state of – well not 'love'; I could not build the confidence to mouth the word – but, what was it, instead? Reinvigoration? Rejuvenation? Optimism, perhaps. Yes, but that word is a bit dull, flat and inadequate. You get 'optimistic' about share prices or your side winning a close game. It's inadequate for human emotion – no, cross that, *emotions* plural. I was discovering that feelings come in combinations and that these may even be conflicting; that joy can be accompanied by fear, every uplifting sensation haunted by awareness of its inevitable end. This ability to begin a dialogue with inner sensations could be thought of, I realized, as a skill and one not encouraged by the culture in which I was raised. English reserve prevents us from narcissistic displays of self-indulgence, but it can also cause us to interrupt our own feelings, whether or not they are communicated to others, such that all deeper sensations are confined to inner rooms and solitary moments, never shared directly with another soul, but only with a symphony on the record player or sought in the metre and rhyme of a poem. In the quiet of a library, we are attracted to the raw, direct expressions of a play or novel, yet recoil at uninhibited drama in our own lives.

There was also, in these weeks of early summer, a sensation close to relief that I could form a friendship on my own merits, in addition to those of convenience forged through a shared experience; and at the ability to expand my repertoire of perspectives and interests and engage in conversations that had ambitions beyond that of careers or gossip. Elizabeth and I had met half a dozen times, in pubs or at each other's houses. I had still not ventured to invite her to an evening dinner, conscious that overly romantic trappings might repel her: *'Dinner means bed,'* Aunt Kath's wise old friend – what was her name, again? – had advised me.

In all this time, however, my form on the cricket field suffered; whether through distraction at new interests or coincidence, I could not say. I still attended weekly net practice at which the batting seemed to go well, but almost every innings ended early, for a variety of reasons. One weekend I reached nearly 30, playing quite fluently, but was then run out. It was more the fault of my batting partner Eric.

'Sorry Col,' he muttered as I walked past him on the way back to the pavilion.

'I forgive you,' I replied. Inwardly I was annoyed, yet with my spirits still generally buoyant in this very different new summer, only mildly.

'Blimey, I wouldn't – if it were me,' he said with a cheeky grin. 'I owe you a beer or three.'

Despite my reticence with Elizabeth, I had developed just sufficient confidence to call on her unannounced once or twice, as I did one damp evening in early June, when cricket practice had been cancelled. She was pleased to see me. There was, however, an atmosphere. Shelley was there, red-eyed.

'Have I come at a bad time?' I asked.

'Yes, well no. It doesn't matter. Come in.'

'Mum's mad at me,' said Shelley.

I was flattered that Shelley sought to include me in a conversation.

'I'm not mad at you, darling,' said Elizabeth kindly. 'I'm just looking after you.'

'She hauled me out of the pub in front of my friends. It was a humiliation.'

'My love, you are under age, and I didn't like the look of those lads who were trying to chat you up.'

'I'm only a few weeks under-age. I'm not a little kid. We were just chatting, just flirting. Men enjoy flirting too, don't they?'

She seemed to be asking me. 'Er, not really, I'm afraid. To a lot of young men it's just a means to an end. They call it spadework,' I added, probably a little too bluntly.

She had been expecting my support, so reacted with dismay. 'This is the worst day of my life!'

'Oh come now,' I said. 'You're only young. You've got plenty of even worse days to come …' Elizabeth flashed me a look. 'I mean… sorry, that came out wrong.'

Shelley marched out of the living room and up the stairs. We could hear a door slamming.

'Well,' I said, 'You've at least given her a room to be able to storm off to. Sorry, I probably said all the wrong things.'

'Yes, probably. Never mind. Don't worry, it's me she's mad at.'

'Well, you are absolutely right to protect her!' I said with force. 'I've spent a lot of time with men in sports clubs over the years and, while some of them are fine lads, others have an appalling attitude to women, I regret to say. Of course, the promotion of casual sex since the Swinging Sixties has made things worse, with young men more free to seek sex without commitment, such that young women have to be much more on their guard. The ancient custom of courtship is now extinct. It has always struck me as ironic that feminists pushing for equality should have exposed young women to additional pressure.'

As I finished this little polemic, which was completely unplanned and rather impulsive, I worried that I might have offended her liberal principles. Instead she observed: 'That is an interesting angle, Colin. It didn't quite happen that way around in the Sixties. The men pushed for free love and the feminists responded, but yes, you have a point.'

She added: 'And perhaps we shouldn't worry too much. It's just a spat, probably. This isn't even nearly the worst day of her life, by the way. When social services found her she'd been living off dry cream crackers in a filthy apartment for three days while her parents were stoned on heroin. Sorry, I've just breached confidentiality with the case notes. Please don't tell a soul.'

'Of course. I'm used to dealing with confidentiality. I guess she blocks that memory out and dumps some anger on to you.'

'Yes, I guess. How do you raise children? Everything you do right is also a little bit wrong.'

'Aunt Kathy had a friend who was a child psychologist. He used to advise: "Don't starve them. Don't hit them on the head."'

'Thanks. Guess I'm doing ok. I just get tired sometimes. Don't you sometimes want to quit virtue? You know, be a hedonist for a few years?' her eyes sparkled a little.

'What, drop out and do LSD?'

'Well, maybe not go that far.'

'Yes, you could end up like Shelley's parents! But how far do you go? How far do you go to entertain yourself, and how far do you go to care about others? And do others even want you to care about them if you're too earnest and miserable? Not you, I mean; "one".'

We were sat side by side on her one sofa, and she had leaned a little closer to me. I got up smartly. 'Shall I make us a cup of tea?'

'Oh, OK, yes. You know where the kettle is? The cups and the tea bags are all out on the side.'

I returned with the hot mugs. 'I've just remembered,' she said. 'I'm hosting a prayer group in an hour's time – though after today I'd much rather share a bottle of wine and listen to Joni Mitchell. Do you want to stay?'

'Um, OK,' I said. 'I don't suppose Shelley will want to join us.'

'No – she can stay in her room and play records.'

The others arrived; mostly Methodists of a kind I found a little over-eager and a bit scary. There were a couple of greying beards, and holy books clutched close to the chest. But they had kindly manners, so maybe it wouldn't be too bad.

As we began, sat in a formation close to circular, on various soft and hard-backed chairs in the living room, we could hear rumblings of a major domestic beginning next door. There were muffled shouts – a female and a male one – with the unmistakeable tone of jealous fury; indistinct but loud through the maisonette's thin walls. A cup or a plate was smashed. It didn't sound accidental.

The theme for the prayer meeting was peace in our world, announced the tallest Methodist with the greyest beard. He clasped his hands and closed his eyes. The rest of us did likewise.

At length he spoke. 'Let us pray first for peace in our community.'

There was a brief period of silence, then the sound of more smashing crockery next door, and the muffled yells of: *'You can take your sorry self round that blonde-haired **## whore and see if she'll do your ##**!ing dishes and your laundry!'*

'And we pray for peace on earth ....'

'At least she and her mother don't nag me all day and all xx!##ing night!' More smashes. The thin living room wall shook briefly.

'... and goodwill among men. In the words of St Francis of Assisi: Lord, make me an instrument of your peace: where there is hatred, let me sow love; where there is injury, pardon; where there is discord, harmony; where there is error, truth; where there is doubt, faith; where there is despair, hope; where there is darkness, light; and where there is sadness, joy.'

*'And you can take your **ing **## and you can shove it up your **##ing arse!!'* Something hard and probably metallic thumped against the thin wall from the neighbour's side. This time I feared it would break.

'We pray for forgiveness, for dialogue, for mutual understanding; and for reconciliation where there have been historic wounds. In the Middle East and in Yugoslavia, in particular.'

'If you were anything like as good at earning a wage as you are at shagging some cheap slag you'd be a XX##ing millionaire by now! Smash. Bang. No wallop, at least.

Elizabeth and I had begun giggling when we shouldn't. 'Corpsing,' I believe actors call it, made worse by the fact that the earnest Methodists remained deep in contemplation, eyes closed, oblivious to the domestic carnage next door. As soon as Elizabeth and I caught each other's eye, we were done for. Chewing at her cuffs and shaking with mirth, she said:

'I'm sorry, I think I'm going to have to attend to Shelley. Excuse me.'

'Let me help,' I volunteered. We gathered in the hall, shaking with laughter. 'Shh!' she said.

Shelley appeared on the stairs, her mood transformed, a cheeky grin on her face. 'I don't think your prayers for world peace have travelled very far today Mum. Not even next door!'

'It's all right for you,' said Elizabeth. 'You don't have to go back in there. Can we come up and listen to music with you?'

We could hear one more terrible smash, then the sound of a slamming door and engine ignition. Meekly, we returned to the living room. The prayer meeting ran its course.

'I thought they'd never leave,' said Elizabeth, after they finally had.

'Should we check on next door? I hope she hasn't been murdered.'

'Colin! Such imagination. But I suppose I'd better check.'

'I'd best come with you,' I offered.

'No, I'll be fine. I know her a little and we shouldn't go mob-handed – will just pop my head round the door; check everything's OK.'

She returned after only a minute or so. 'Yes, all fine. Bit embarrassed and keen to see the back of me. You see, Shelley – it's trying to save you from a life with a useless man like the poor woman next door that I intervene.'

'I know, Mum. S'pose I ought to be grateful.' She looked up with a smile. 'You know so much, being old and wise and all that.'

'Hey, less of the "old" thank you very much!'

The prayers for peace had at least worked at home.

'I'd best be going,' I said. 'It must be Shelley's bedtime?'

She gave me a look. 'I'm 17, not seven! But nice to see you again Colin.'

'Yes, nice to see you too.

''Bye!' she said as she sauntered back up the stairs to her room, leaving Elizabeth with me.

'Well, see you when I next see you – if not before!' Pleased with my feeble joke, I smiled.

Our eyes met at that point, and she gave me an affectionate look. Her fingers brushed against mine, probably accidentally, but I enjoyed the sensation. Perhaps I could kiss her? Perhaps we were finally … well, connecting. Is that the right word? It had been so long, I did not know the signs, the feelings, the cues or the clues. I trembled, hesitated, then leaned in and to my astonishment she did too. We kissed for a few moments; mouths closed then opening as her body softened. I felt desire and something more; an exhilaration, laced with a sense of home-coming, nostalgia, a personal affirmation, all of which combined to produce an emotional release that left me close to tears. I wanted more. I so wanted us to abandon this tiresome English reserve, and tear off our clothes and make love, just do it, anywhere - the floor or the sofa, up against the wall. But though Desire bravely fought its duel with Fear, it perished gamely. I could not be sure of Elizabeth's reaction, did not wish to appear too rough or too forward. How far you take matters with a woman is one thing; how far you go with an intellectually superior former nun who probably represents your last chance of marital union in your entire life is something else entirely. And so fear of The Rebuff reappearing with commensurate recognition of how high the stakes had become, I withdrew and bade her goodbye. She gave me a faintly quizzical look as I left; not sweet but perhaps bittersweet. Ambiguous, I decided.

13

In the fast lane

The sun shone hard. I rose early and looked at the morning scene with pleasure from the bedroom window. It was the pinnacle of the year: the second Saturday in June and my favourite opponents, Caribe, were coming down from east London for an all-day game, starting at 11.00.

I arrived early, and so had some of my colleagues. Derek and Tony were in eager discussion with the groundsman, out in the middle. There appeared to be an altercation, and the groundsman, a genial chap called Arthur, threw his arms suddenly up in the air and walked proudly off. I approached the square.

'Shit,' said Derek, looking aghast at the strip of earth prepared for the game.

'We're done for,' said Tony.

I stared also, knelt down and pressed with my knuckles. It did not yield. The reflection of the sun glinted off the smooth, polished surface. The few blades of grass were straw-coloured and pressed firmly into the ground. I felt a surge of exhilaration.

'That cretin Arthur!' said Derek. 'What is he playing at? He knows this team. They've been coming for years. They've got Trinidad's ex-opening bowler and he prepares a strip where it'll come off like shit off a shovel. If we bat first it'll be over by half twelve and half of us in hospital. Arthur's sacked.'

'Probably revenge,' said Tony.

'What for?' asked Derek.

'Practical joke at the start of the season,' said Tony, chuckling.

'Oh yeah!' Derek said, grumpily. The club had spent several thousand pounds, and Arthur many days of work, to relay the square in March and April. Eric and Andy 'Pike' Peacock, after a few beers in The Swan, packed some loose soil into a wheelbarrow, pushed it out on to the ground after dark, and created fake mole hills on the edges of the revamped pitch for Arthur to discover in the morning. They stayed to record his reaction on a camcorder.

As the one lover of fast bowling the team, I stood up and beamed. 'Cheer up Derek. At least we go out in style. Anyhow, Jeffrey didn't used to open for Trinidad & Tobago. His family's from Dominica, and they moved to London when he was a kid. Though he did open the bowling for Essex Seconds for a couple of seasons.'

'Like that's supposed to cheer us up. Anyway how do you know that?'

'He's a friend of mine. A good Christian.'

'Doesn't bowl like a fucking Christian.'

'Oh, come on Derek, he bowls in the corridor. Test of skill.'

'I got some chin music last year, as I recall.'

'The occasional shortish one is a perfectly legitimate shock tactic for a quick bowler. You're all padded up and helmeted these days, anyway, like a knight in armour.'

He muttered something inaudible.

'Maybe they won't show,' suggested Tony. 'Maybe Jeffrey's injured, or not playing this year.'

Derek did not reply. We heard a scrunch of tyres in the gravel car park and turned to see a couple of saloon cars pull into our car park. Jeffrey was the first to emerge, and seemed relaxed and athletic in movement.

'Well then, let's hope Bodger was sober last night.'

At which point Eric appeared, looking dishevelled and hung over, confessing he'd yet to have breakfast and was there time to grab a burger from somewhere. More gloom in the ranks.

'Blimey, I'm starving,' he said.

'You can't possibly be starving,' replied Derek, poking him aggressively in his widening beer belly. 'Why can't you just draw on your reserves? You've got enough to last a fortnight there.'

He stroked his widening girth with pride. 'Got to keep me strength up.'

'Bollocks. The last thing you need is another meal. Take a look in the mirror! Don't you think food is the way you got into this state in the first place? Anyway, start of play is only half an hour, and this is a strong opposition.'

'Let's hope I win the toss,' muttered Derek as we retired to the pavilion. He didn't, and 20 minutes later Tony and I were walking out to the middle.

I took guard and waited for Jeffrey to begin his run. I was more nervous than I had admitted to my team mates, but I knew my adversary well. He was stocky and muscular. His run-up was not long nor fast, so his speed could come as a surprise to the newly acquainted. The first ball this morning was high and wide and I let it go. The second pulled me into the shot, left me and leapt a little, missing my gloves by a fraction. I could hear the fizzing of the seam whirring through the air as it passed with alarming speed, and I wondered if my captain's pessimism had been overdone after all. Jeffrey whistled silently through pursed lips, and turned back to his mark. I gave him a steady look and calmly redrew my guard in the hard earth. The next delivery came into me. I stayed steady, watched the ball, and sent it hard down. It bounced extravagantly and the bowler himself caught it. The rest of the over was wide of the mark. The sun became exceptionally warm, and the ground unusually silent. Few of my team mates seemed to be watching and the visitors' family members were still unloading picnics from the car boots. Tony played out an over from the other opener, a medium pacer who seemed accurate but only able to swing the ball in.

Jeffrey ran up again. Once more I was beaten by the extra pace, the ball bouncing past the edge of my raised bat. It was a loose shot and I was lucky to have survived. I allowed myself a few paces up and down and settled myself. The next was quicker still. I prepared to turn it away but it thumped into my chest. A few of the opponents, including Jeffrey - who I knew would buy me a rum later to compensate - approached to reassure themselves that I was unhurt. I pretended I was not and carried on. The next delivery was also venomous, but I was beginning to adjust to the pace of the pitch and I met it firmly, sending it away to the fielders. The next was fuller in pitch, inviting the drive. It is possible, after such a pounding, to be fooled by a weak delivery, and scarcely to believe the evidence of one's own eyes. For a very short space of time I hesitated, but instinct had taken my left foot into the correct position and, following through, I felt the middle of the bat meet with the ball. At such speed it took only a steady push to send it flying past Jeffrey's boots and up against the chestnut tree by the sight-screen. He sent a short one down which bounced high and I cut at the ball, failing to control the shot completely, but managing to reach the boundary again.

I prodded the faultless surface with my bat and breathed a sigh of relief, but also reminded myself that I had only eight. 'Eight,' I said to myself. 'Not even double figures. Concentrate, now. Watch the ball: hit it.'

The last ball was down the leg-side. I edged it safely away to the fielder on the ground's edge and trotted a single. I failed to score from the next over, which left Tony to face Jeffrey. He looked nervous, prodding the ground ferociously as he waited. He swished at the first and missed, trying hard to look dignified in the process. The next was of fuller pitch and I knew what was going to happen before anyone else. With a deathly clatter the middle stump was sent cartwheeling towards the wicket keeper and the hapless Tony walked hurriedly off the field.

Greg was next in. He was good enough to have represented Sussex at youth level, but was vulnerable to pace. Today he began quite confidently, however, and took a few singles. Within a little while I was facing Jeffrey again.

There followed a torrid over; the fastest of his spell, and I managed to make contact with only two of them. One of the deliveries I did not actually see the ball at all, but just heard it thump into the wicket keeper's gloves. I gave the bowler a nod of praise.

Greg wandered down the pitch between overs. 'Why don't you wear a lid?' he asked me, pointing towards his crown, as though there were some ambiguity as to where protective headgear might be positioned.

I pulled a face. 'It would weigh me down. Slow me down. Gary Sobers didn't even wear a thigh pad.'

'Gary Sobers was a genius. No offence.'

'None taken.'

In his next over he tried me with a bouncer, and I ducked safely underneath; then with a fuller pitched delivery, which he got wrong. I knelt down and with a crack! sent it skimming through the offside. He gave me a little nod of appreciation, returned to his mark, and promptly fired in the quickest of the day. It beat me hopelessly and rapped me on the pad. There was a huge shout. Too high, I thought; too high - it was above the knee-roll and I was jumping. Yet still my pulse raced and the sweat in my gloved palms turned cold as I landed, propped myself up with my bat and looked up. It was their umpire - a bookish, bespectacled man sporting a trilby who looked a little too young to be retired from the game. He gave me a studious look before politely shaking his head and murmuring 'Not out'.

I scored heavily from the other bowlers. The problem was that Jeffrey was able to work his way through my colleagues. Greg was out; then the captain. Derek typically batted a little higher in the order than his ability strictly merited, on account of the fact that, as captain, he picked the batting order. His election as captain each year was generally unopposed, however, on the grounds that it is actually quite a time-consuming task to select the players, ensure transport for away fixtures, risk unpopularity by selecting the batting order and so on. Del-boy was all-too happy to assume the responsibilities as he loved the status it gave him. Plus he lacked other interests and his wife Carole was quite keen for him to be busy with matters that didn't include her. He was a very good fielder and made good judgements when it came to choosing who to come on to bowl. So all in all, a pragmatic choice.

Eric followed Derek and was a little unlucky – connecting fairly well with a short ball but caught in the deep. Hector came out to join me. 'I'm feeling lucky, Col,' he announced. 'I was just about to cross the road this morning when a sixth sense told me to stop. In that instant a huge lorry came past. So I've escaped death once today already.'

'Just concentrate and watch the ball,' I instructed.

Hector proceeded to do this rather well. He tended to point both feet towards the bowler as he essayed a shot, in contravention of good coaching and common sense, but he overcame this handicap by watching the ball ferociously, like a hawk. On this occasion, with the ball flying fast but normally straight, it was a reliable virtue. He stayed a while and Jeffrey began to tire. When I thought I had reached thirty-five or so my team mates in the pavilion began applauding. I had 50. Our scoreboard at the time did not record individual scores. It is always a good sign if you have more than you think.

I trotted up the pavilion steps for lunch, suppressing a smug smile as I joined my team mates. They were still animated over the events of the morning.

'But with all due respect, Derek, you're talking complete bollocks,' Tony was saying. I erupted into laughter with my colleagues.

'Well that's not much respect at all, then Briz, is it?' yelped Bodger, doubled over with mirth. 'That's got to go up on the Quotes board.'

'No, but he ain't listening,' Tony proceeded to explain, perplexed and unaware of his oxymoron. 'He's talking complete bollocks. With all due respect. We can't beat this lot with pace - no offence, Dale, you're a good bowler. But they're used to it, aren't they? We should have a go at them with spin.'

'What? You and whose army?' said Derek. 'It's not as if we've got Shane Warne in the team, exactly. Pitch is flat as a board. And fast.'

'We've got Kennel. And Pike. Maybe Bodger can bowl his leggies.'

'You have got to be kidding me!' said the same Bodger. 'I'm not having this lot cart my bowling into the next village.'

'We might not have the same problem anyway, this year,' Derek said. 'I don't recognise half the team, and they look a bit older. Their best bat, comes in number three normally, I haven't seen. Plus they've got an old guy in the ranks. Maybe 180-odd might be enough.'

'It's good to talk high tactics, ain't it?' said Bodger sarcastically. He hid his intelligence with his dissolute life. 'They should put you lot on the telly.'

'No, but I reckon we're doing OK,' said Derek, who thought that captaincy was about winning arguments. 'We've been unlucky as well. Just think: if I hadn't got that bitch of a ball, and if the pitch had eased out sooner, and if your shot hadn't gone to hand.'

'Yea Del,' quipped Eric. 'And if my aunt had bollocks, she'd be my uncle.'

Derek 'Hrrmphed' rather loudly and muttered something about positive attitudes. I took a shower to wash away the rivulets of sweat, ate a sandwich and drank a pint of tea.

Tony's pithy observation did subsequently appear on the Quotes board inside the Home dressing room, along with other memorable aphorisms from the tacticians and philosophers of our club, such as – this from Derek Cooper in 1992: *'The batting this afternoon can be summed up in just one word: Complete and utter shambles.'* Unimpressed, Briz would mutter most times he caught sight of his own, for many years afterwards: 'But he was talking bollocks. You had to have been there.'

I got changed again, ready to resume my innings, and wandered back into the bar area, looking for another cup of tea. Derek, struggling to conceal his envy, commented to me: 'Didn't think you'd still be there come lunch. I got a snorter.'

'Yea,' I replied. 'Got a few myself. Great, though, isn't it?'

I rubbed my sore chest gently and wondered if a rib was cracked. He stomped grumpily off.

'Col!' complained Bodger, who was sat to one side of me.

'Yes?' I asked.

'You'd make a better door than a winder!'

'What? Oh, sorry,' I said, moving away from his line of sight of the television. 'Money on a nag this afternoon?' I asked.

'Bad Boy in the 1.30 at Ascot. Five to one. Trainer knows the course like the back of his hand.'

'Good luck.'

'Oh, and Col,' he added.

'Yea?'

'Well batted, mate.'

'Thanks,' I said, beginning to grin. 'Thanks a lot.' I moved back to the bar, picking up a slice of Battenburg and a smaller cup of tea. The hot milky liquid spilled over the rim of the little rickety cup and mildly scalded my squat forefinger that scarcely fitted in the tiny handle. I retired to the bench by the wall, and slumped on it, back propped up against the wall, smelling the almonds and cigarette smoke, listening to the conversation of Bodger and Greg.

'Any joy last week then?' asked Bodger.

'Brilliant mate. Best ever. We're in a bit more money this year - took the girls and sat in the grandstand, 'stead of on the Downs. Atmosphere was electric. Only thing to ruin it was Gary's horse romping home not mine. Couldn't care, though, really. Got pissed on champagne for the first time ever. Like bleeding royalty. How's you mate, anyway? How's the missus?'

'Not bad. She's over at Guildford today with 'er mum. Retail therapy.'

'Sounds serious, mate. Can you afford it?'

'Yea – it was my idea. I keep telling 'er to treat 'erself.'

'Get over!'

'No! Straight up! It's Julie I've got to worry about. Kids today want it all. She'd happily spend it all on them.'

Then I noticed Elizabeth, who must have entered the pavilion quietly. I looked up in surprise, failing to catch her eye. I had had no idea that she knew anyone connected with the club, yet she appeared neither to notice me nor to seek me out. She bought a ginger beer from the bar and began talking to Dale, who was slouched, wearing tee shirt and track-suit bottoms, feet up on one of the bar's squat plastic chairs. I was appalled, though even at that moment of sudden emotion I nourished a silent pride at the evidence that the youngster, by not bothering to change into his cricket gear, showed confidence in my ability to stay at the crease.

I wandered over to them. 'Hello,' I said.

'Hello,' replied Elizabeth, calmly and with faint warmth. Even Dale grunted a little and almost looked at me.

'Are you free after the game?' I asked her.

'Yes,' she said, with an ambiguous smile.

'I'll see you then,' I said, and felt constrained to move away. Discomfited, I wandered about the pavilion briefly before fetching another tea. A few minutes later Elizabeth disengaged herself from Dale and came to me.

She said, 'Actually, I'm free now, if you want to say something.'

'Well,' I began, looking up at the clock. 'Not now perhaps. I'm back on in five minutes.'

She looked a little disappointed and said, 'Fine. I'll see you later.' She walked off.

Jeffrey did not pose the same threat after the break, and his captain gave him a rest. I was seeing the ball so well that I could start to hit the good balls as well as the bad. But, despite the exhilaration, I began to feel achingly tired. I kept calling for drinks, and turning down runs that should have been easy to take. The 22 yards became 44, then 100. Only in the few seconds of the bowler's run-up and as I faced the delivery did I not feel this debilitating tiredness.

Hector was out, and I began to lose partners at the other end. Dale came in. He gave what I thought was a nod of appreciation as he approached me and said, 'You've got 92.'

He went to his end and took guard. His first ball missed the bat, but not the stumps, and he loped off with an aloof air, as if his failure were just an act of guile. The next man was the last; Andy 'Pike' Peacock, who was useless. The bowling switched ends. I glanced the first towards the boundary, where it was fielded. Andy came storming enthusiastically down the pitch. 'Get back!' I yelled, turning down the easy single that would have forced him to take strike and almost certainly end the innings. I had to keep the strike – not just for my sake, but for the team's. Like an obedient puppy he retreated. The next delivery was in the same slot but I made better contact, sending it firmly past the umpire to the pavilion gate. Four runs.

I leant on my bat and surveyed the scene. The faint breeze had disappeared and a haze developed below the horse chestnut tree and pushed out across the common. Flies buzzed around. I caught sight of Elizabeth again, which surprised me, as I had presumed she had left earlier. I steadied myself to assure myself of the identification, but there was no doubt. My batsman's eyesight, after all, is excellent. Her slight figure was dressed in simple white blouse and green slacks. She stood facing away from the pitch and towards the church. I gasped and felt the sweat on my brow, pausing to wipe it with my shirt sleeve.

The next delivery was a good one. I came forward, but too late, surprised by a little extra pace. It flew off the edge of the bat and I groaned despairingly inwards. But I had reckoned without the extra bounce. I turned to see the ball fly from the tips of the slip fielder's hand and race towards the boundary. A fielder chased and dived to stop the ball, but merely sent it crashing into the tree. There was a yell from the pavilion, then another shout and, more gratifyingly still, a cheer and some applause from the visitors' families. I had 100; the first of the season and the first any of us had posted against this opposition. I planted my flag in my Everest, and looked up, feeling a surge of pleasure at the applause, and the evident joy of the visitors' families. Elizabeth had gone.

The opposition's turn came to bat. Derek was quickly rewarded with his policy as Dale made early inroads, sending three of them back within half an hour, though one of the opening batsmen scored freely.

'You see,' Derek said triumphantly to Tony as we gathered for a brief chat at the fall of a wicket. 'I told you we had a chance.'

'Yea, well,' said Tony. 'Don't get carried away.'

'Cheer up, mate. Anyway,' he added, looking towards the pavilion. 'Looks like we've got granddad now.'

A white-haired, lanky gentleman strolled towards the crease with langorous movements and settled, waiting for his delivery. He took guard left-handed, seemed unusually calm, and I noticed that he kept his head very still, without apparent effort. Dale sent down an easy-paced delivery and the batsman played defensively, sending the ball to me. It came inordinately quickly and stung my hand as I picked it up.

The next had a similar result, but with just a little follow-through the ball flew faster, seeming to gain in pace as it went past me. I hoped my team-mates did not rate this effort as a fluke. Dale's next effort was perfectly good - indeed quite unplayable to a normal batsman - but this chap was not normal.

He played it near the top of the bounce – 'on the up' - with perfect timing and sent it flying for another boundary.

He continued in this vein against all the bowlers. The very timbre of the ball striking the bat had a superior quality. Never once did he show the merest sign of effort, nor permit a bead of perspiration show, nor betray a trace of emotion. Some of my colleagues committed the conceit of chasing the ball after it had gone past them in futile gestures, but I just stood and admired. Within an hour and a half the game was over.

'Well, Colin,' said Jeffrey as we stood in the bar and I poured some beer into his glass from my jug. 'We had a good contest today.'

'I've been waiting a long time for this,' I said proudly. 'My first jug against you lot in years of trying.' It was customary for a successful bowler or batsman to buy beer for the opponents. 'Best ten pounds I ever spent.'

'Ah but Colin,' he said, slapping his hand on my shoulder. 'Think what it is like for me: I have still not got you out.'

'You won't get much sympathy with a grin like that,' I said. 'Have you not, really?'

'No,' he said emphatically. 'Never. You know, Colin is a good name for you, because you are just like Colin Cowdrey. You look a bit like him and he could play the quicks.'

'Funny you should say that.'

'Anyway,' he added, lowering his voice with fake threat. 'Next year we are bringing a leg spinner.'

'You wouldn't do that to me, would you?'

'We would,' he said, grinning again. 'Top-spinners, googlies, you name it.'

'We have to have a contest,' I protested. 'It's got to last all day.'

'We had a contest today,' said Jeffrey innocently.

'Well, yes, until Gary Sobers came out.'

'Ha!' Jeffrey threw his head back and roared with laughter, then looked about himself mischievously. 'Rumour has it Colin,' he told me gravely, 'That he is a cousin.' He started laughing again, slapping me on my shoulder.

'He was the real article, as far as I could see,' I said, with fake annoyance.

'The look on your skipper's face! It was worth it!' he exclaimed.

'Will you be back next year?'

'Well, I hope so, but I'm not getting any younger, nor are my team-mates, and we're struggling to get the next generation to come along. Young black kids in London just want to play football now.'

'Really?' I asked, surprised and upset.

'Yes – cricket's too time-consuming; plus we really struggle for facilities and grounds. You have to have a ground to play in the leagues. And the ones who are better at sport earn weekend money playing football. Take my lad Benjamin – he has the making of a good fast bowler, but he's in the first team now at Dagenham & Redbridge. Gets a wage, too. Season starts in July! No time for cricket with the old man!'

'You must be proud though.'

'Oh yes, as long as he keeps up his studies. He wants to go to Birmingham University to do sports science.'

'That would be great – best of both worlds,' I agreed, nodding with approval. 'But listen, if your club's struggling, why don't you move down here? Play for us!' I said in a burst of enthusiasm.

He gave me a look of distance and sorrow, and I suddenly realized the enormity that such a change would mean for him and his extended family. For me, racial prejudice was something that I read about in the newspapers; for Jeffrey it had probably been an every-day experience in 30 years of living in London. The difficulty of moving to a near all-white town in Sussex was something I was left to imagine. I recalled with a shudder the occasional disparaging comments that I overheard in the pub and the dressing room from time to time about young black men; probably said more in ignorance than with malice, yet disturbing nonetheless.

As the opposition got in their cars, I noticed the flecks of grey in the hair of some of them. Was this to be the very last fixture between our club and Caribe? It had been established decades earlier by the respective club presidents, now both deceased, who had served together in the British Army. The problem with needing a ground for home fixtures reflected the drive for leagues for the amateur clubs, in parallel with a push for more professionalism in the county game. In England, until around 1960, there was something known as 'amateur' status in the counties. Gentlemen who were wealthy enough to play distinguished themselves from the professionals who earned a wage, and considered themselves higher in social status. Until the 1950s you had to be an 'amateur' to captain England. At the level of the clubs, especially in the south, there was an emphasis on 'friendly' fixtures honouring the amateur ethos and the spirit of the game, rather than leagues where the emphasis was more upon winning and chalking up points. Amateur status introduced an absurd sort of social distinction, so it had to go. But as ever with social progress, the baby was thrown out with the bathwater. Out went the old school tie, class distinction and much nonsense; but also out of fashion was walking when you were out, applauding your opponents, and generally playing to the spirit as well as the letter of the laws of the game. As Jeffrey's lament indicated, the drive for leagues was depriving some of the poorer teams of some of their most attractive features. Perhaps the next generation of city kids would have preferred football anyway, but this trend can hardly have helped. Many inner-London teams were 'wandering sides' – they could not afford their own ground, so depended on away fixtures with clubs like ours. Through the 1970s and 1980s these fixtures thrived. It would be a grand day out, with the families often coming along with picnics in a coach. It was an irony, but the anti-elitist campaigns were helping to terminate some fleeting but genuine encounters across the social divides.

It wasn't just me; an entire way of life was approaching its close of play: friendly fixtures, 11.00 starts with a break for lunch, West Indian sides coming down from London with proper fast bowlers. I was 44 and creaking at the seams. Maybe I'd be in the seconds next year, or even the thirds, who played their fixtures out of town on a recreation ground that I'd never even visited. I shuddered.

I arrived home, anticipating a late-night whisky to finish off the perfect day, in a tranquil half hour savouring the day's achievement. I called Elizabeth, partly, it must be admitted, to boast, but also to ask which service she might be attending the next day. She sounded oddly out of sorts, and less than delighted that I had called her, a reaction which disturbed me the longer I stayed awake, suddenly unable to enjoy or see purpose in anything. She is bored with me, already, I decided. The day of great triumph ended in bewilderment, renewed melancholy and a sensation almost like fear.

14

Heresy in the garden

The first thing that I remember the next morning as I awoke was that I could not move. The next was that someone was using a weighted mallet with which to pound the front, sides and back of my skull simultaneously. My body tensed rigid with alarm at this unexpected paralysis and I made a great effort to relax it. I essayed a tentative movement with my left leg, hoping to swing it over the side of the bed, but the merest movement sent a grinding pain in the bone on the outside of the knee, which then shot upwards and downwards along nerve and muscle. Dimly aware of advice that being motionless made such muscular atrophy worse, I defied instinct, summoned my will and forced it to over-ride the democratic instincts of my nervous system. After much effort and cursing I was sat up on the side of my bed. As soon as I did so, blood poured through the huge purple bruise on my chest where I had taken the blow.

Unwonted as these sensations were, I could account for them. Every ache and pain bore with it a memory of the day before. The chest; the heavy legs from the sprints and turns; the aching head from the beer and whisky that I had foolishly drunk instead of water or juice.

I had hoped to attend the 9.30 service, the one that Elizabeth preferred on the occasions she attended All Saints, but it had taken me over an hour to rise, shower and breakfast. Instead I went to the 11.00, often a rather gloomier event with fewer communicants, and no one whom I knew. It was almost a sad day, despite the huge achievement of my innings the day before. Only by recalling the very best shots – the straight drive that rattled the sightscreen, for example – could I stave off the worst of the returning melancholy, and only temporarily. I was glad I was not due to play that afternoon.

By the Tuesday, I felt scarcely better, and attended the doctor's surgery in the hope that some exotic ailment could take the blame for my general malaise; but there was none. The GP, a slip of a girl who must have been not yet 30, worried openly about arthritis, and asked me about my age in the tone of one inquiring after a sick relative. I called Derek to advise him that I would be unavailable for either the Saturday or the Sunday. He too made a quip about my age; something about 'granddad needs his afternoon nap'.

I lay in lazily on both days of the weekend. One of the few advantages of living alone is that you can let chores slip if you want to, and put up with the dust and the long grass, or with eating out of tins, for a day or three. By the late afternoon of the Sunday I felt recovered, and wistfully regretted having opted out of that afternoon's game, especially as the weather was beautiful: warm without being oppressive; just a hint of a breeze. I thought that I should at least attend Evensong. In previous years I would quip to a vicar or fellow parishioner that 'there were more in the choir than the congregation', and at the time it was an exaggeration. These days, however, it had become true. Few churches maintained an evening service, another symptom of the long, slow decline of the Church of England. It meant that the few folk attending may come from neighbouring parishes, and on this occasion, it included Elizabeth.

After the service, tentatively, I invited her to mine for a glass of something, and she agreed with surprising eagerness. I could have asked her about the coolness towards me that I had detected at the pavilion the week before, but as she seemed discernibly happier at meeting me that evening, I assumed there was nothing to discuss.

'I'll have a gin and tonic,' she said firmly and uncharacteristically. It was still warm into the evening, one of those June dusks when it stays light until 10. We sat on the steps that led down from the French windows to the lawn of my garden. It was west-facing and the sun was on our faces. A few birds made the occasional lazy attempt at song, but had lost the fervour of spring. There was an electrical lawn-mower buzzing next door.

As she sat down she emitted a huge sigh, far deeper and longer than one would expect from the lungs of a petite lady in early middle age, before declaring. 'Oh, that's enough church for a while, I think – I might take a couple of weeks off!' Her exasperation surprised me, as she had given no hint at the service or on the way home.

'Anything about this evening's psalms or readings?'

'Oh no, I'm just having one of my periodic bouts of irritation at organized religion. Just seems so ritualized and pointless sometimes.' She paused, then said: 'I don't mean to alarm you.'

'That's OK,' I said. 'I've always found the people who make the best company are the religious folk who have doubts, and the atheists who wonder if there's something more.'

She thought about this. 'That's not a bad guide for people to keep company with,' she said. 'Don't be afraid to say what you like to me by the way, Colin. You know, you do look at me sometimes like I'm holy.' She made it sound like an accusation.

'Well you are, aren't you?' I replied.

'Good God, I hope not!' she said with force. 'What do we mean by "good", even?' she paused another long while, looking away towards the back of the garden, towards the thickening silver birch and the mound of compost at its feet. My spirits fell. It was going to be a heavy conversation.

I had no idea what to say, so said nothing.

'I had a sheltered upbringing,' she continued in a gentler voice. 'In Shipbourne, from the cricket ground, which is a little out of the village, you look up at the church and the houses, which are on a slight rise. On a misty day in the evening, it looks like Camelot. I grew up with the feeling that the world outside was dangerous. I suppose my parents fostered this impression, God bless them. Anyway when I went to inner London or India or Africa later in life I set out with the feeling that I was a true missionary, trained in altruism, bringing hope into dangerous parts. I must have looked terribly earnest and frightened at times.' She smiled and looked down. 'But I did listen to the people I met. I didn't just talk.' She looked up at me. 'Most people aren't interested in ideas. They get on with life. I've seen good things and bad things, but the things that stick in my mind are the irrational lengths ordinary people sometimes go to to help each other out. Most people are nice.'

While she talked I had been looking sometimes at her, sometimes at the garden, tracing circles with my fore finger around the glass rim. 'All this just supports my view of you,' I said. 'I've been waiting all my life for someone to explain things to me; the reasons for everything. You just go out and discover. I just think about it. And I work as a solicitor. Most people I see aren't nice. Just the religious ones. And even some of them ....'

She paused a long while before replying, but whether it was to absorb my observations seemed unlikely. She appeared rapt in her own line of thought. After a while she looked at me briefly and then towards the rear of the garden once more. At length she spoke. 'When I was in the convent I became friendly with Sister Angela, and we used to – well, not exactly rebel – but send ourselves up and the seriousness of our devotion and studies. We used to play,' she attempted a mischievous smile. 'A game we called "heresy". Except that, strictly speaking, it wasn't heresy at all.'

'What did it involve?'

'We would read to each other the most shocking, violent parts of the Bible. We would take it in turns, and read it quite formally, you know 'A reading from the Book of so and so' and close it with "This is the Word of the Lord". The trouble is, we had rather more material than we bargained for. I used to say to Angie "If our congregation knew this was in here they'd stop coming". Of course all the scholars have answers for it all; and there's an underlying ethic that is evolving, laying the foundations for law and moral conduct, but I sometimes wonder. I sometimes wonder if those scholars are right. There's stuff that would make Quentin Tarantino feel a bit queasy. For example, the Lord commands Joshua to eliminate the entire population of Ai, including women, children and livestock, because they were unbelievers. Jehu is commanded to wipe out the descendents of Ahab; trample his wife to death and throw her body to the dogs. Then he rounds up the worshippers of Baal, herds them into the Temple and has them killed. Then there's the Book of

Revelations in the New Testament, which is positively scary, and a bit bonkers.' She paused a long time.

'Even Jesus isn't nice the whole time,' she added, glumly and reflectively.

'Isn't he?'

'No.'

'Oh. He upset his mum, I suppose.'

There followed another lengthy silence with which she appeared comfortable, but I, not. At length I spoke. 'The most telling thing was that you said how the congregation did not know of these barbarities in the corners of the old book.'

'That makes it worse, doesn't it?' she asked. Her voice was raised slightly, and I became aware of a hint of attention from the couple next door, who had been sat at their outside table, drinking martinis. The lawnmower from the garden on the other side had paused, allowing them to be able to overhear. 'It smacks of concealment or censorship.'

'No,' I suggested. 'It means the sound teaching has survived the test of time. 'Do unto others; Blessed are the meek, the Psalms, the Proverbs, guidance on charity from Isaiah. The Ten Commandments.'

'Yes, I suppose so.'

'But you have a point. I have sometimes wondered why the evangelicals bang on about the Bible so much – it's more like our guilty secret, at least parts of it. You could imagine a writers' meeting on The Good Book. Chairman of the editorial committee says something like: "Some really strong ideas here, good teaching and fine writing – but it's way too long, there's far too much violence and it needs a few jokes. We need a bit of light and shade; changes of pace".'

'So,' she said. 'What's your dream team? Who would you have on your editorial committee?'

'Oh I don't know – Mark Twain, Groucho Marx and Dave Allen,' I suggested. 'And they should be supplied with a bottle of finest malt whisky for each meeting.'

She did not reply straight away, and seemed to lose a little animation. I gauged from such a subdued reaction that she had been hoping for a rather more serious suggestion. Unfortunately, I lacked knowledge of the principal ideas of leading moral philosophers and theologians; or indeed, other salient facts about them – what they were called, for example. I had always been rather intimidated by abstract thought, preferring to stay with the solid facts of history and the law. I was not able to offer her the intellectual stimulus to which she was accustomed, and I was not confident I was offering much in the way of emotional support for her crisis of faith, either. Instead I asked her, 'You know the infamous passages well. What's your favourite?'

This had a better effect. She smiled, looked downwards as if with guilt at taking pleasure in the Holy Book, and said, 'John 20, verses 11–14.'

'Read it.'

She did not need to go indoors to fetch a copy, reciting from memory: 'Mary stood outside the tomb crying. As she wept, she bent over to look into the tomb and saw two angels in white, seated where Jesus' body had been, one at the head and the other at the foot. They asked her "Woman, why are you crying?" "They have taken my Lord away," she said, "and I don't know where they have put him." At this, she turned round and saw Jesus standing there.'

She became briefly lachrymose, shivered, and turned away. 'Even that's not terribly holy,' she muttered. 'I'm sure some psychologist could explain it all by saying how it really means that I was looking for a man when I was young but pretended that I wasn't.'

'Baloney!' I exploded. 'What do psychologists know?' I said. 'It is a great mistake to assume that because there's a whole industry and literature about some novel topic you have to conclude "Oh, there must be something in it". Psychology and evolutionary theories are just attempts to reduce humanity to some simple, mechanical explanations. You know the kind of thing - Michelangelo painted the Sistine Chapel because his Dad beat him up and he was trying to attract a mate. It's just a licence for philistines.'

She appeared mildly amused rather than either shocked or in agreement. 'Interesting historical facts – who are the psychologists who've posited that Michelangelo suffered child abuse and had ulterior motives for artistic expression?'

'Oh, I don't mean that precisely; it's just an example,' I said with irritation.

'Well, it's not a terribly convincing example then, is it?' she asked.

'Well, I suppose not,' I replied. 'You win.'

'A discussion doesn't have to be a contest,' she said. 'It's not a game of cricket. Psychology isn't some threat to the human soul – it's just a line of scientific inquiry.'

I fell silent and she took pity on me. She asked, in a gentle fashion: 'What's your favourite part of the Bible?'

'The garden at Gethsemane,' I replied straight away. 'I always had so much empathy with the disciples, as I'm so fond of a kip myself. And it always struck me as the most haunting image. I've imagined it as a painting. One figure taking up arms against a sea of troubles while the rest sleep.'

'Sister Angela and I used to say to each other: "Still reading the Bible?" and the other would reply "Yes - for my sins. Ha ha ha." It was funny the first time. Our favourite books were not religious. After playing 'heresy' we would read Brontë to each other, and discuss which sister we were most like. I used to call her Anne and she would call me Charlotte.'

'That sounds about right,' I commented.

'If you think that I am self-deprecating, you should have met Sister Angela, my Anne. She often used to sing the first verse from 'My Song is Love Unknown'. It was her motto, really that line: 'And who am I/That for my sake/My Lord should take frail flesh and die?'.'

Elizabeth looked by turns deeply sad and then suddenly brighter. She said: 'She had the most acute sense of guilt I have ever known – she was capable of feeling remorse over things that she *might* have done – as if there were less virtue in resisting temptation than in never falling prey. If she were watching a television drama and something terrible happened, she would vaguely feel that it was her fault. People can be queer. Of course, we wanted an Emily,' she continued. 'And after a while we got one.'

'An Emily wouldn't stay in a convent for long.'

'No. She didn't.'

'And nor did your "Anne" – that is to say, Sister Angela?'

'She died.'

'Oh, my God,' I said quite abruptly and loudly, as though the tragedy had just occurred before our eyes.

The lawn-mower buzzed more loudly as the neighbour came nearer, pushing the machine up against the roots of the bordering hedge, causing a rasping noise as the blades cut into the bark.

'And I left the order shortly after. I just broke down. That's when I met Godfrey – on the retreat. The problem, of course, was not that I had a crisis of faith, but that I didn't – well, I hadn't at that point; it came later. It was hard to explain to myself or to anyone that I left because I had lost my soul mate.

Faith ought to be deeper than that! A vocation should come from the spirit, not rely on friendships for support like a crutch. Do people just "do" religions because they enjoy them, and quit because they cease to?'

'You haven't quit,' I replied. 'Your life is one of service.'

This did not have the comforting effect that I expected and I fell silent. It is frustrating that while one's flippant comments can be remembered for years, a phrase that one imagines expresses the apt sentiment and appropriate phrasing is lost to the air like bubbles. It was some months, or perhaps years, later that I wondered if my use of the word 'service' fell upon her ears more as a dreary prediction than a compliment.

'There was something else; something major. Some*one* major,' she confessed. 'He wasn't a cleric, in case you're guessing,' she said, with a ghost of a smile. 'We didn't used to see many men, of course, but I worked in a day centre. I didn't fall for an old drunk either, though I did save a young volunteer from doing that, poor girl. Probably the best thing I did there.

'He was the coordinator. I think he quickly saw me as the steadiest of the volunteers and placed a lot of trust in me. We became quite a team; quite a ... partnership. Lunches in the Italian cafe round the corner. I didn't always wear my habit, and even when I did I forgot about it and forgot that I might look actually fairly comical, pretending I was flirting, and that he was actually interested.

'It was,' she paused, her voice finally breaking after maintaining an impressive fluency, 'un...unrequited.'

I could hear a robin twittering in the tree. I clumsily put my hand on her shoulder. 'It's funny how the word "requited" only ever applies to love,' she continued, giving a philosophical gaze at the trees. 'Sometimes I find the cliché very comforting - you know, it gives me something in common with millions of other women, which is quite reassuring for a freak like me - but at other times I want to scream at how all of my emotions and experiences and things that went right to the core of my being get picked up and bottled in a jar called "unrequited love".

'Of course I saw my spiritual guardian; my mentor, and told everything - well, nearly everything, and I had long discussions about the impact on my spiritual life, but by that time I was too confused about what the word "spiritual" meant to be able to make progress. That's why Godfrey was such a help. He didn't see it all as some terrible problem to be solved, but just listened to me, and believed me. No one else could see why I had to leave the order, though they were terribly kind.'

At last I said something. 'Perhaps love never goes completely unrequited, or unrewarded,' I offered, with a vague hope that the idea might hold merit, rather than on the basis of any sound knowledge.

'Yes, that's what he said too. Something about karma.'

'Oh – I'm not sure unrequited love helps you become calmer,' I said.

'No, I think what he meant was…' she paused and held back from further clarification, kindly declining the opportunity for condescension. I realized my aural miscomprehension some hours later. '….that is to say,' she continued, 'All experiences stay with you, in some way or another, I guess, and in the people you've had relationships with,' she added. 'You can forget events, but not emotions. They become part of you; like your hair colour or your taste in music.'

It had become chilly and we we went in. She didn't want another gin, so I put the kettle on. She stayed quiet and calm and stared out of the bay window as she sipped her tea. I felt useless sitting next to her on the sofa, undecided whether to look at her or not, and desperately thought of something to say.

She put her hand on my thigh, in a familiar manner, as if she had done so often. I felt moved and clasped her hand with mine. For a moment I felt excited also, and drew her close. Then I remembered who she was; and I remembered who I was, and let her go. She seemed displeased neither by the embrace nor by its end, but seemed rather soft and malleable; quite content to be manipulated by me. We did not look at each other, but rather stared out of the window, my hand lingering on her shoulder, but otherwise not touching. After a long silence I gathered myself and stood up.

'I'll make you another tea,' I said.

'Thank you,' she said, and looked briefly up at me, and then paused another long while. 'I must be going now.'

'Must you? Won't you stay for something to eat?'

'No, I, er, appreciate everything, Colin. It's nice to be able to talk.'

I wondered briefly if she was discreetly begging that I urge her to stay, but I decided that her resolve was genuine. 'I'll see you out,' I said.

It was on the point of leaving that she made a gesture, half towards me. I thought she had lost her balance. I steadied her, and with what I thought was a friendly smile, bid her goodbye. She gave me the most peculiar look, and left.

15

The dinner party

Dale appeared at a practice, for the first time since before the season started. He had played in a few games. Again he refused to return my greeting. Again he directed a few deliveries at me rather than at the stumps, but I played them well. I was quite pleased that Hector, with his slow spinning deliveries from a bowling action that caused him to appear like an eager boy performing circus stunts - his straight longish hair projected upwards by the friction of his upper arm brushing past his head in a rapid, swirling motion - presented me with more difficulties, though I rather doubted that Dale noticed this. He turned at the end of his run for his final delivery to me and ran with extra pace, his face, mildly reddened, was contorted with effort. The ball travelled rapidly but was overpitched. I waited until it was under my nose and drove it hard back towards the bowler, at about shoulder height. He watched it pass him with an expression of disdain, not bothering to essay a catch. I sauntered out of the net and began to unbuckle my pads.

'I'm going to give up cricket,' Hector announced afterwards in the pavilion bar. 'Another nought on Sunday.'

'Don't be silly,' I said. 'You're mainly a bowler anyway.'

'Every time you think you've got it licked; you've learned your lessons, that it can't trick you any more, it comes back with a vengeance. Slap!' he said as though onomatopoeically, though I could think of no sound in the game quite like that. 'It brings you back to earth.'

He slurped his drink and looked meaningfully at it.

I asked: 'So why did you come to nets?'

'I always come to nets.'

'You said you were giving up the game.'

'I might give up playing matches, but I would still come to practice.'

'Well, what would be the point of that?'

'I could still enjoy the bowling and the batting and trying to outwit someone, but not have to face… to confront… *death* – you know, getting out.'

I looked at him. He was most earnest. 'It's like life in this way,' I suggested. 'Some people seem destined to stay at the crease, no matter what, and you have a feel for it, despite their mistakes. God's on their side. It's like that with life. Someone lives through the trenches; someone else chokes to death on a fish bone.'

'My uncle was in the Warsaw ghetto,' said Hector. 'Walked all the way to Switzerland disguised as a woman; lived on wild rabbit and scavenged fruit, and one night he hid in the carcass of a horse to escape the Nazis. Lived to be 93. Smoked 40 a day. Only one of his immediate family who survived, mind you.'

I added: 'I read an obituary of a Great War soldier a couple of years ago. Bertie Ratcliffe, I think he was called. Was left for dead on the battle field, picked up by Germans going through the corpses, taken as a prisoner of war, escaped through Holland back to Britain, returned to the trenches. Died at the age of 98. Credit to the German surgeon who operated on him, mind.'

Hector took a long draught of his drink and so did I. 'You wouldn't last long if you tried to give up cricket,' I predicted. 'Derek would be on the blower to you every other day; "Can you play? Go on, we're one short in the seconds". Do you really want his nagging voice on the phone three times a week?'

'No, I suppose not.'

'Well, you have two choices.'

'What are they?'

'Carry on playing, or emigrate.'

'Oh. Best keep on playing then, I suppose. Another drink?'

Elizabeth had come into the pavilion and said hello to me cheerily enough, but again made an approach to the surly Dale. Or perhaps he had wandered over to her.

He seemed to be looming above her, as a tree hangs over a bench, and was terribly close. I detached myself from Hector - we had been joined by others - and walked towards them. Dale glowered as I approached. Elizabeth shied away and we escaped to the corner of the bar.

'Was he menacing you?' I asked.

'Not at all,' she replied. 'He was perfectly nice.'

'I find that difficult to believe. He's so surly and bad mannered.'

'I swear to you he is not,' Elizabeth said, with surprising resolve. 'He is perhaps a little insecure.'

'Insecure? Are we talking about the same person? He's the most arrogant youth I've ever met.'

'You sound very cross, Colin. What are you really angry about?'

'I'm sorry,' I said. 'I probably sound old-fashioned, but Dale represents everything I dislike. Ever since punk rock it has been fashionable to be rude to people. Every time I say something like that people think I am making some political statement and that I'm an arch reactionary. I'm not. It's nothing to do with politics. I just don't see why dressing badly and swearing represents progress.'

'Nor do I,' she answered tetchily. 'But you have to be fair to people. Have you actually heard Dale swear?'

'Well, no. He hardly talks. He is sullen and rude. That's a perfectly fair summary.'

'He says about you that you never say hello when he greets you.'

'Me? That's him!'

'That's what he says.'

'Anyway, how do you know him?' I asked irritably. 'Why do you bother?'

'He's started dating Shelley.'

'He's *what*?

'She's 18 in a couple of weeks' time, for God's sake. He's only 20 himself. He's hard-working and honest. He's polite and doesn't take advantage.'

'How do you know?'

'He does play cricket.'

I sulked and stayed silent for a while. 'Maybe it's just me then,' I said. 'I must remind him of his headmaster or something.'

'Anyway, I would ask you to put your prejudice aside because I would like to invite him and Shelley to dinner. And I would like you to be there.'

I accepted, of course. Even if I felt as though I were making up the numbers, it was an invitation from Elizabeth and I was in no position to begin turning those down. One or two excuses for avoiding the event did cross my mind, in the days afterwards, but there was no serious prospect of my declining. On the day itself, despite my disinclination I left work early and washed and dressed in plenty of time. A gentle breeze blew through the light evening, and the house martins chirrupped as they fed their young in the nests beneath the spacious eaves of the old house. My spirits sank at the thought of the trial ahead but, looking back at the sad, dingy cream wallpaper of the hall as I prepared to cross the threshold, I felt also an air of melancholy and loneliness that pervaded the house, which I thought I had banished since the spring, and left.

His hair was hanging ever lower over his dark eyes, in two sweeps of black. His long frame was slouched on the bean bag. Shelley, by contrast, was animated, and fussed over him with more attention than he merited, fetching tea and asking was he all right. Elizabeth was in the kitchen, cooking. I said 'Hello,' (at least this is what I recall - he may have disputed this later). I received no reaction from Dale and while Shelley made a gesture that appeared a prelude to speech, she followed this with a quick glance at her boyfriend and she remained quiet.

After half-crouching above the settee I changed my mind and walked the short distance to the kitchen, issuing a sigh which must have been audible, despite my best efforts. Elizabeth looked at me with a frown and placed a tureen and four bowls on a tray. She replaced a silver strand of her brownish, shortish hair that had fallen onto her forehead, while looking downwards and a little self-consciously. She wore a flowered frock beneath a patterned, frilly apron and looked quite attractive in her domestic state, despite her modesty and nervousness.

'Let's go through,' she ordered.

We sat at the table. 'Did you buy that sweater in Brighton

that you wanted, Shelley?' Elizabeth asked.

'Yes,' she said, glancing downwards, and then up at Dale briefly, flicking up her long fair hair over her shoulder with a quick, twitchy movement, before stooping again over her soup.

I made an effort and said to Dale. 'You went to the same school as Eric, then?'

'Yea,' he said, looking downwards. 'A few years later than him.' He picked up a roll and broke it in two, holding each half between thumb and forefinger. He ate a little and then picked up his wine glass and drank. He said to Shelley: 'Did you get that CD?' I saw him grin for the first time.

'Yea,' she said, and giggled.

I looked at Elizabeth, noiselessly asking for support. Not appearing to receive any I cast a glance at the small living room. The large cheese plant was the only item that gave an appearance of permanence. There were no pictures affixed to the wall; only a miniature poster, stuck in a photographic frame that rested on its support on the mantelpiece. It featured no picture; just Victorian lettering that bore the legend 'Much is required from those to whom much is given - Luke 12:48'.

'Shelley,' Elizabeth said. 'Please don't hunch over your bowl. Could you go and fetch some more rolls, please?'

She was surprisingly obedient and placid, though retained a smirk on her face. As she returned, Elizabeth asked her about whether 'Sally' was having an affair.

'Who's Sally?' I asked.

'It's a plotline from Coronation Street,' she explained. I wasn't sure if she was trying to draw the young woman into the conversation, or simply annoy me.

'You watch soap operas?' I asked.

'Are you trying to show disdain in that tone of voice?' she replied.

'No, I am trying to conceal it.'

'So-called soaps can make for fine drama – in serial form, with a cliff-hanger, that's how Dickens wrote.'

'That's a ridiculous comparison,' I said. 'It's like saying the duet from the Pearl Fishers is a song. I'll Tell You What I Want, What I Really Really Want is a song, therefore the Spice Girls are the Verdi of the modern age.'

'The Pearl Fishers was by Bizet,' she said pointedly, enjoying her little triumph.

'Yes, well. Was it? Well, same point.'

'I think what we've just learned Colin, is that you seem to be better acquainted with the oeuvres of the Spice Girls than Bizet or Verdi.'

Shelley chuckled at that. She was proud of her Mum.

At the end of the course Elizabeth gathered the crockery and took them away. I helped her, trying to conceal my haste. I let the dishes clatter in the bowl rather too much. Everything felt wrong.

We returned. The main course was pork and apple sauce. The meat was hot, the mashed potato soft and creamy, with thick gravy that invaded the hollowed scoops.

'Do you like the wine?' I asked Dale.

'Yea,' he said. 'Is it Piesporter?'

'Yes,' I said, surprised because he could not have seen the bottle, which remained in the kitchen.

'I've been grape-picking there,' he said.

'Was that fun?' I asked.

He suppressed a laugh, looking with dark contempt at a man who had never done a full day's manual labour. 'In the evenings. You get tired by then. The Alsace is the last on the tour - you start in Roussillon in September. The sweet wines you pick in winter. Braziers between the vines and snow on the ground. The leaves have gone. All the grapes are rotten. All of them. The wine fetches a fortune in the shops. Ten pounds for a bottle of fermented mould.'

'Were you away for a while? Working as you travelled?'

'Travelling as I worked,' he explained. 'I saved a thousand pounds. Switzerland was best. The thing to do was earn there and spend it elsewhere.'

'Et as-tu appris le français?'

'Bien sur. J'ai passé quelque mois sans parler anglais,' he responded without hesitation, with dogged fluency and a strong accent.

'What was you saying?' asked Shelley.

'What *were* you saying,' I corrected. I could sense Elizabeth's alarm, but my tone was not so harsh and she remained quiet.

'What was it then?' she asked me, wanting to smirk again but catching herself with an intake of breath and a glance at the forbidding Dale.

'That Dale went a few months without ever speaking English,' I explained.

'How did you manage that, then?' she asked him, with more curiosity than admiration.

'You don't understand a thing at first, so you just guess; pick up clues from what people are doing. If you're working you have to learn. You don't have any choice, really.'

Elizabeth asked: 'What was your favourite part of France?'

'I bet you're thinking "Cannes or St Tropez",' he said. 'But no. I would say Burgundy. The Côte d'Or. It's different from England 'cos the posh people really work. This proprietor, he's worth a fortune, gets up before us, sits at breakfast with us, and works like a n-… like, well really hard, 14 hours every day, and he's about 110. Great guy.'

I noticed how he lightened considerably when talking to

Elizabeth; more even than with Shelley, with whom he was a little awkward.

'Did you ever think of settling in France?' asked Elizabeth.

'Yea, I could get on there. But I could only get casual work. To get proper work you have to be French and have the right qualifications, which I couldn't afford to take.'

So the surly one spoke French. It was a revelation, though hardly a transformational one; though I hoped for her own and for Elizabeth's sake that Dale treated Shelley well. It did not occur to me then, as it might have done, that perhaps I could be surly, too.

16

The attic

My meetings with Elizabeth became less frequent during July. She was often busy with marking papers, or charity work. We had a couple of enjoyable drinks in the pub, but on one or two other occasions she cancelled a planned engagement with me at short notice, citing an issue that she had to attend to either at the school or with Shelley; on one occasion, to be at the deathbed of a beloved aunt. During this time we discussed many topical and church issues. I had thought that she enjoyed this as much as I, but Elizabeth seemed to become sadder on each occasion. On one occasion, for example, we discussed women priests.

'I suppose I shouldn't be surprised that you oppose even the most rudimentary equality in the church, if you don't like inclusive language,' she said provocatively. She seemed to be trying to adopt a devil-may-care attitude; that this is just a battle of wits, but her emotion sometimes betrayed a touch of either fear or anger by a trembling of her fingers and effort to control her voice.

'Progress isn't linear,' I replied. 'It's not measured by notching up rights like beans in a jar. And I don't object to women priests per se.'

'You don't?'

'It's the theology that goes with it. It's the pretence that the liberal state is superior to the church; that the church is just another voluntary organisation that must follow the mores of the political class; of people who may or may not have its best wishes at heart.'

'Why do you attend a liberal church like Godfrey's? Why don't you attend a high church, or campaign for a repeal?'

'That's the whole point,' I replied. 'I don't mind if the vicar is conservative or liberal. I don't care how he votes. Or how she votes! I want the church to be a refuge from campaigns and causes. Why does everything have to be so political? I see politics as a sub-category of God's stuff, not the other way around.'

'Well yes, maybe we are getting a bit secular at the edges,' she reflected. But she seemed stung by the force of my opinion.

She changed the subject, offering to put some music on. She knew I loved Handel, Scarlatti, Bach and Albinoni, but dared to challenge me. 'Do you have any Greig or Mussorgsky?'

'Good lord no,' I replied. 'Nothing modern. Well, maybe some Elgar and a few others…'

She rolled her eyes. I saw her do it.

'When Scarlatti composed his sonatas,' I explained, attempting a justification. 'Music was seen as sacred. People actually believed in the soul, deep down, and composition was a form of prayer. Since then there has been the tendency for too much ego, and experimentation for its own sake. Well, in my opinion.'

'I'm afraid the name Scarlatti only reminds me of some terrifying piano lessons,' confessed Elizabeth. 'I had a scary music teacher.'

Nonetheless, she relented, playing the Goldberg Variations to prevent grumpiness on my part. She observed: 'This is actually a modern, free-form style, if you think about it.' I didn't rise to the bait.

We were sat in my roomy living room. At length, she became restless. She wanted to explore the old house, and I gave her the full tour – for the first time. The attic room was big enough to walk around in and there was a permanent, if steep, wooden staircase that led up there. The early summer sun through the skylight picked up the thick dust and sent it scattering.

'There are old Victorian wooden toys and everything, Colin! This is a delight!'

I thought of her sparsely furnished flat and felt guilty.

'These pictures are beautifully framed,' she commented.

'I note you didn't say "beautifully painted",' I replied, gently.

'I'm sorry; no, they are. Who were they by?'

'My mother's mother Alice. She painted the whole time, apparently. She suffered from what used to be called bad nerves, and painting was the only distraction that worked for her.'

'Do you remember her?'

'No, she and granddad were killed by a Doodlebug.'

'Oh, my word! How terrible! Your family has been dreadfully hit by tragedies. Colin, how awful!'

I looked at her pained expression, and felt mournful. 'I've never thought of it like that,' I said. 'The events have all been quite separate in time. I suppose my parents and grandparents were all cut off at their prime, or thereabouts. I've often thought about it. I sift through the evidence and pick up crumbs of comfort. They never knew the pain of old age. They all went quickly. They knew their place in the world and never had their rightful authority questioned. Their sudden passing makes the whole era more completely in the past, and more completely separate from the present. I was born in 1952. Yet sometimes I feel the most poignant nostalgia for the 1940s or even the 1930s. I look at a magazine from that era; or at one of these paintings, and think "That was a good time to be in Britain, in spite of her perils". I'm glad I was, and I think I was.'

'Do you believe in a soul?'

'I suppose I do, but I've never been convinced that God knows my thoughts. That must sound arrogant. And my dead relatives are absent from this house, as far as I can tell. They're not here, and it's been many years now. Practically all my life.'

'I'm sorry,' she said softly. 'I've brought all this up.'

'Don't be. It's not grief, you see, not any more. But it is loss, of course.' She waited for the next word, but there wasn't one. She picked up one of the watercolours and looked at it. It benefited from a longer study because Alice's draughtsmanship was very much better than her colouring, so that while an initial glance jarred a little, the scene was authentic. I loved the casual manner in which she portrayed a blazer; a young woman in long white dress and round, white hat of the inter-war years; the running board of a sports car at the edge of a deep meadow edged with cypress trees, as though this were commonplace, without being able to realise how impossibly exotic and remote it became just one generation later.

'Everything was so different then,' I commented.

'I wonder,' replied Elizabeth. 'We talk so much about how things change. We talk very little about that which stays the same, which are the more important things after all – love, respect, care, children. Family. These people in the painting may have had less money if they had lived after the war, but I do not suppose that their lives and loves would have been that different. They might have been happier. They might have liked the Beatles and the Bond movies. I love to look at Victorian photographs of people. You can always see a face that you had seen in the pub the day before. The differences are just fashion. Superficial.'

There was quite a long silence. 'So you lock these paintings up in the attic,' she added.

I thought about this for a long while. A gasp of air from the open hatch sent a swirl of dust, large golden globes in the streaming sun, spinning violently and shooting upwards. 'I don't really spend much time on the appearance of the house, or sorting out all these relics. I suppose there are antiques and everything. It always becomes the task that is endlessly deferred to another day.'

She sat down on a rug that lay on an old suitcase. I sat down opposite, on an ageing trunk. Much as I had begun to love her, I wanted her to leave this attic.

'Who's this?' she asked, after leafing through a shoe box full of old photographs.

I looked at the faded print and my heart thumped twice, violently. 'Um,' I said. 'Brigid.' I took the photograph with more than natural alacrity, serving only to heighten the curiosity I wished to avoid.

'Was she a girlfriend when you were young?' she asked, playfully.

'Sort of,' I said, blushing. 'I'm not sure we ever called ourselves boyfriend and girlfriend. We didn't used to go to the pictures or anything like that, but we did used to meet.'

'But it is kept in a frame, with an old diary…' she began, then fell quiet, aware of her intrusion.

'Let's go down,' I said, with too much haste and a little irritation. She followed me silently. I made some tea and brought the tray through. I had felt an urge to be quiet and alone but as I sat down I began to talk and to continue.

It felt as if emitting one sentence constrained the next to come, in Pavlovian fashion.

'I have too many memories,' I said. 'But too few achievements. I am burdened by these echoes; these images. There is one that feels ancient, and yet it was only a few years ago; and it is merged vaguely with one from childhood; and there is a memory from school years that is not like a memory at all; but like an emotion that is still present.'

'What is that?' she asked.

'I was in the maths classroom. The master had just left and we were chatting. Jackson was the lad of the year; the looks, the intelligence, the sporting ability, the contacts. He came in and told the others: "Morison's going to be allowed a go in the sports car..." I still have this feeling that, perhaps next year, I'll have a go in a sports car and have a girlfriend. Next year I'll prove myself. This feeling is almost as though my life is still in the future.' I paused for a while, extremely uncertain of Elizabeth's reaction, then added: 'I'm sorry, it sounds silly. I cannot imagine how I began talking in this maudlin fashion. I must be a dreadful bore.'

She said simply: 'The English are the only people to apologise when they start to talk about interesting things.'

17

Let's go sledging

I had returned to playing after a couple of weeks' break from tiredness and bruising, but the runs were hard to come by again. My century at the Caribe match represented more than half my tally for the entire season, so I wanted to practice and be in the runs again. For a Saturday game in mid-July I arrived early at the ground before a league match on the Saturday, and persuaded Hector to bowl me a few in the nets so we could both limber up. Once again, Eric was a little late, arriving just ten minutes before play was due to begin, and his appearance caused some alarm. He was sporting a lustrous purple bruise near the top of his nose, he was dishevelled and he seemed out of sorts. It was a fine but breezy day, his hair had gone uncut for a while, and was made more disordered still by the wind.

Tony, however, was breathless with excitement. 'Haven't you heard the story?' he said to the rest of us as we gathered in the changing room.

'No,' replied Derek.

'Let me tell it, then,' said Tony. 'We were in The Swan last night. Anyway, this posh bloke starts getting arsey; claims he was next in line for a round. Bodger says no I was here first. Etcetera. Etcetera. Bit of banter. Who are you anyway? Matey ends up saying "Do you know who my dad is?" So Bodger says "No. And last time I shagged your mum she said she weren't too sure either." Cunt punched him in the face.'

'He got beaten up by a public school bloke?'

'Tidy punch, credit due,' said Bodger. 'Must be all that rugger.' He was grinning, but rather weakly; certainly less enthusiastically than the norm – generally he loved being the centre of attention and the subject of some tale from the night before. For most of the lads, the latest escapade and quickfire repartee simply added another colourful chapter to the folklore of Eric 'Bodger' Gray, but I was simply looking at a dazed and confused young man, with an injured and possibly broken nose. Getting into pub brawls tended to become a habit, even if extenuating circumstances and pleas of being an innocent bystander could be made for each incident. It concerned me that, in his mid-30s and with a wife and young children, his weekend drinking sessions showed no signs of abating; almost the opposite.

Despite his injury, he batted number 5. We had lost three quick wickets so it wasn't long before he joined me in the middle. It was the end of the over as the wicket fell, so I walked over to greet him. 'Are you OK?' I asked.

He said 'Yeah,' rather vacantly, before sauntering to the non-striker's end. Sensibly, he was wearing a helmet, to protect the injured face from further damage; and perhaps also on this day out of a desire for a little privacy, and protection from verbal spats – known as 'sledging' in cricket – that opponents on a cricket field, even at this amateur level, would engage in from time to time. Such comments rarely bothered me, and I never spoke back. Generally, I just took it as a compliment if they were trying to get under my skin. On one occasion, the chatter from the fielders backfired completely. In a low-scoring game, early on in my innings, I fended off a delivery from a quicker bowler. The fielders, clustered round the bat, over-excitedly shouted to their bowler: "Good line! You've got him in trouble there!" I had actually found the delivery quite comfortable to handle and thought: 'Well if that's his best ball, I'm going to be fine.' I relaxed immediately and I finished not out as we won.

On this occasion the opposing team, perhaps sensing a little wariness in Eric's body language, tried to put pressure on him with fielders close to the bat. One was just a few yards in front on the off side, at silly point – able to make eye contact in between deliveries should the batsman cast his look in that way. Despite his condition, he got off the mark and made a reasonable start.

For myself at the other end, I was disconcerted. Two batsmen at the crease are constantly chattering with each other, mostly about how many runs to make if you've hit the ball and it's not going to reach the boundary. We have our own code and jargon: 'Wait! Come one! Quickly! Looking, looking; OK, come two!' There are rules of thumb: if a fielder has to turn and chase the ball, you can almost certainly complete at least one run. If he is running in towards the ball to pick it up, there's more risk. The old saying 'Don't run on a mis-field' has many exceptions, because it depends on which type of mis-field – should the ball disappear through the fielder's hands at pace, you can probably safely set off. There are also sound principles about whose call it is: if in front of the batsman taking strike, then it's his call; if it goes behind him and behind the wicket, the onus falls on his partner. On this day Eric was almost mute; I had to make his calls as well as mine. Between overs I came down the wicket for a chat, but he had little to say.

Then the sun disappeared behind a cloud. The shade beneath Eric's helmet visor diminished and the fielder at silly point spotted the bruise. 'Hey, this one's been hurt already: smack him in the face Hurricane!' (The store of nicknames for fast bowlers has a limited range). Eric went mad. He didn't say anything, but I saw the white heat of anger in his eyes. Sure enough, the bowler pitched the ball in short. Eric aimed a hook shot and missed by a long way. There was another short ball – he flashed at it, and made contact with just the edge of the bat, sending the ball skywards. It landed safely, without being caught and went for four runs, but it was a lucky shot. The bowler made sure to remind him that he considered it a fluke. More heat to the fire.

Anger is an unpredictable beast in sport. Too much can lead to poor judgement and reckless risk-taking; but just occasionally it can be channelled creatively. It is rarely as disabling as excessive caution. On this occasion Eric was so enraged as to be scary. After a couple of streaky shots, he hit some genuine ones. Through sheer force of adrenaline, anger, innate ability and chutzpah, he played himself into form. Some shots were audacious; almost self-destructive, as if he were trying to get out – stepping away to give himself room and then smashing an accurate delivery right in front of the stumps away through extra cover. Outrageously, on this occasion, they came off. The fielders, intimated by his rage, began to step back and give us more room to pick up singles and twos. I was prepared to take a back seat in the partnership; startled and dazzled by his bold bad shots and his bold brilliant ones, but increasingly concerned for his mental state. Eventually he skied a delivery and a fielder caught it safely. Had it been the individual misguided enough to have sledged him about the bruise, I'm sure he would have been too nervous to have held on to the catch. Eric was out for 57. He had to walk past me on the way back to the pavilion. I said well played. He said nothing.

In the pavilion bar after the game, he cut a morose figure; this normally gregarious individual sat on his own; a depopulated circle surrounding him, like a spot of detergent repelling grease. I ventured to sit opposite him at the small table.

'Do you fancy a pint?' I asked

He looked up. 'I'll have orange juice and lemonade.'

I returned with the drink. 'I see England are struggling in the test match.'

'What'd you expect?'

Long pause.

'I thought you batted well today.'

He looked up and looked me straight in the eyes. Said nothing for quite a while, then: 'Thanks, Col.' Another pause. 'Listen, I'd better head home.'

'Sure.' He emptied his sweet fizzy drink in one go, placed the glass on the table, picked up his kit bag and walked out of the pavilion door, down the steps and headed home. His path took him across a section of the outfield. Some children were playing their own game of cricket, with small bats and a tennis ball. They ignored Eric and he ignored them, as their game continued around him. His large bag was slung over his shoulder and he pressed on, in a dead-straight line, head down.

18

’fessing up

It was a week later that I next met Elizabeth. I sought her out with eagerness after the morning service. She was talking with the same elderly woman she had been in conversation with on the day of our first meeting the autumn before, but this time was less inclined to leave her company. I tried to catch her attention once or twice as I talked with Godfrey about cricket.

I caught up with her as she was walking towards her car.

‘Do you want to come to the pub later?’ I asked.

‘No, Colin,’ she replied. ‘We drink too much.’ She said ‘We’ but she meant ‘You’. She added: ‘Let’s just walk in the common a little while. It’s a nice morning.’

She said as we reached the common: ‘Who’s Brigid?’

‘Is that what is bothering you?’ I asked, beginning the sentence with polite surprise but sadly ending it with a little disdain. It occurred to me for the first time that she was probably a virgin.

She had a custom of hesitating before she spoke, when

it was a matter of import, as if frightened of stuttering or misusing her vocabulary. An imperfection would appear on her brow; not a furrow, exactly, more a soft indent, like a dimple, in the centre of her forehead. It seemed to reflect pain rather than puzzlement. It appeared in the few moments before she replied and provoked the familiar sense of unease and suspense in my own heart.

'Well, it's not really my business, I suppose, and it was a long time ago, but I'm only human so I'm bound to be curious.'

'Well, I don't know,' I replied. 'A slight sense of shame, I guess. I probably didn't treat her well, but then I didn't know how to treat a woman. I still don't. I don't suppose many young men do – or middle-aged men for that matter.'

'I'm sorry – I'm bound to be curious about what happened. It's exciting to discover someone's romantic past!' she asked.

'With Brigid?'

We sat on a bench on the common. The sun broke through and it was comfortable to sit for a while. I began to tell her.

There is an exquisite quality to an erotic dream, or a long-remembered romantic interval, that cannot be quite matched in new experience. Perhaps heaven is a spark within us; a memory of the womb, not something other-worldly.

She was newly over from Ireland. I remember my first sight of her in the pub garden because the sun was shining on her black, long, curly hair and on the few freckles on her nose and cheeks. She was pretty, but in an old fashioned sense, with rosy cheeks and an ingenuous smile. In the Edwardian age she might have won a beauty contest, but at the time she and I turned 20 it was fashionable to have straight hair, a pallid complexion and a cynical attitude. She was not 'cool'. I rarely attracted the attention of women; when I did so, she was often not English. I have guessed that as a youth I must come have across as dull and old-fashioned to local girls, but that I could – on a good day – appear to be a distinguished and intriguing young English gentleman to a German, Irish or Danish woman. Brigid took a shine to me straight away; flirtatious, tactile, friendly and expressive. I was astonished and excited.

It was my first day of a salaried job, and the senior partner Alan had taken me for a pint. Beginnings always seem remote. This one now feels as though it were from a former existence. The very tenor of a location which later becomes familiar is, in the memory of one's first encounter, alien and quite divorced from that of all subsequent recollections of the place.

I have never felt that life is short. I am not so young, so I cannot be accused of the youthful arrogance that lends itself to feelings of immortality. A sense of the enormity of a human life derives from the very remoteness and multitude of memories, even now, at what might reasonably be guessed must be a little over half way through my allotted span.

Brigid and the garden are the most distant of all; more even than Uncle Gerald's batting lessons, Aunty Kath's bakewell tarts or my parents. Although time passes quickly, many memories are impossibly remote and I ache, wishing they were closer, and actually wishing my end were nearer; horrified that these distances will actually grow. Life is nasty, brutish and long.

Our encounters were intense, and our communication non-verbal. I did not talk of her to anyone else. It was as though what we did was so completely a matter for the two of us only that no one else must know a thing. Only years later did I realise, with pain and guilt, that what I had fancied as spontaneous and romantic gestures might have come across to her as furtive or even squalid.

It was one of those rare occasions where the group next to you in the pub strikes up a conversation quite naturally, and neither party is bothered in the slightest. Indeed, even Alan seemed quite charmed by the lively group of art students. They invited us back for the evening and I alone turned up.

Later, in their shared house was where she showed me her room, and where we started to kiss. She tasted of lemonade, as she did not like to drink. The events are remote but I can summon the emotion at will. I recall the pant of desire as I began to glimpse her body, though I feel it through my nerves and not through my memory. Afterwards there must have been disappointment, but this I can only construct from events. I can feel it no more. There is a story I have assembled from memories like bits of schrapnel.

She was more beautiful naked than clothed. She had little sartorial style, opting for shapeless cotton dresses and rarely bothering with make-up, but was relaxed and sensuous when clothes-less. She had delicate, freckled skin; soft breasts, a little flesh around the tummy, and slender legs. She had a relaxed, warm look in bed; looking up at me adoringly with trusting green eyes. She made me gasp with delight and awe with the astonishment that she desired me.

We always met at her room. I only once or twice invited her 'home', and never when Aunt Kath was there.

There is a sorting-out that the memory performs. We imagine that some events will leave a lasting scar yet they quickly fade; while others grow and dominate the mind. I shrank away from Brigid, thinking that it was just a secret experiment that would leave no emotional mark and not require explanation or justification. Yet, despite only having met a dozen times or so, I thought of her much, much more than I did Mary, with whom I had been planning marriage; and I thought of Brigid with the most intense tenderness, affection and regret. Why was this? Lust is completely different from love. Isn't it? Our love-making was at once more forceful and more delicate than with Mary; more raw and more subtle; more physical and more emotional; the more intense, perhaps, for being so completely tactile, never accompanied by observation or plans.

Perhaps I could have loved her; perhaps I actually did. Perhaps I could have grown up and put into words what I felt. Through embarrassment and guilt I said nothing and she concluded that I felt nothing - with relief, I thought, but with pain also, I have realised, with the long cold stare of hindsight.

I want time to stand still in respect of people I have not seen for a long time. If I were to meet Brigid again I would expect her to be the same age. I have occasionally imagined us married and fancied that the union would be joyful. Time cheats. It presents opportunities we are not ready for. It pushes us on when we want respite and trips us up when we want to move along. One expects to encounter deep emotion in life; to be so completely in love that it tears into your heart and guts; to be filled to the core of one's being by a sensation so powerful it shakes your spirit and body and one cannot begin to address another matter. What no one tells you is that when this happens you may not be aware of it until years later, and that you brush over the feelings and deny them to yourself. No one tells you of the risk that your emotions, and your awareness of them, may be strangers to one another. Instead, the true emotion may trickle through the layers of porous rock over the years that follow and settle in a subterranean reservoir, slowly rising.

'Well,' I said after telling her much of the above story – with rather more shyness about the physical details, while making it clear that our relationship had been sexual. 'I'm glad I told you.' I recognized immediately that I was rather too self-congratulatory, given that the confession had had to be prised out of me.

'She was young and just over from Ireland,' Elizabeth observed. 'Didn't you worry that you were taking advantage?'

'Well, actually not at all. I was caught up in the passion. Plus I was very naïve myself. I was a virgin before we met – she was not.'

'So, when you criticized young men for wanting sex without commitment, and said the Swinging Sixties were to blame, your code didn't really apply to yourself?'

Ouch.

I hung my head, too ashamed to defend my conduct. 'It just didn't feel like that at the time,' I said quietly and feebly, hands trembling. 'It felt natural, equal.'

'Sorry,' she said. 'Perhaps I went too far.' She did not sound terribly apologetic.

19

Shall I go ?

Just a few days later, she did call, and invite me round. She had left a message on the answerphone, during play on a Saturday afternoon. I avoided church on the Sunday, played the afternoon game, and waited until mid-evening on the Sunday before replying, still stung by her rebuke. So I visited the next day, after work.

As soon as I arrived, however, she seemed ill at ease in my company. I sensed her disappointment as Shelley, who had been visiting and was sat with a cup of tea at the dining table as I first arrived, announced she was leaving to meet some friends, leaving the two of us together. Her increasingly charming young foster daughter departed.

She asked Shelley, trying not to sound desperate: 'Why don't you stay with us for dinner – something nice and nutritious – then go meet your friends later?'

'No, thanks Mum. We've agreed to meet at that new pizza restaurant.'

'Oh, Ok. Do you at least want a drink here before you go?'

'No – thanks all the same. Gotta fly – running late now. Love you!'

She tore out of the living room with indecent haste, opened and then slammed the front door. Elizabeth insisted on watching Coronation Street, which she knew I hated. Her dismay at being left with just me was evident. I read the newspaper, trying not to be distracted by the mournful theme tune of the TV drama, and the whiny self-pitying characters with their affairs and their jealousies. I held the broadsheet up in front of my face, to eliminate any chance of the television images reaching my gaze. I began by turning the page quietly, but confess I began to rustle them a little more often and a little more noisily than was strictly necessary, generating (I imagined from behind the paper) a scolding look from time to time. It may have been my imagination, but I thought I detected the volume on the television control being nudged a little higher, as part of an aural arms race. I backed down first, folding up the newspaper as softly as I could and sat quietly.

'Shall I go?' I asked.

The question seemed to surprise her. 'No. Stay for some dinner. I've prepared something.'

We ate well. She had prepared a delicious casserole that she re-heated. The conversation, however, was stilted:

Some no-go areas had cropped up in our conversations. The number seemed to be increasing. We couldn't talk about education, because I wanted a return to grammar schools. I sympathized with Northern Ireland unionists, she favoured the nationalist cause. On economics, we would blame respectively the unions and the capitalists for high unemployment. Even a comment on how the geraniums had opened early that summer risked a heated debate on the reality of climate change caused by CO_2 emissions. Eventually I asked: 'Could you pass the salt, please?'

'Of course,' she replied. 'Though too much sodium is bad for your diet.'

'Well, at least you don't want me killed off young,' I said.

More silence. I picked up on something I had read in the newspaper, about a much-publicized exhibition of documentary photographs.

'Photography is bunk, isn't it?' I asked, hoping for a non-political debate that would take us away from personal matters. 'I mean, real painters spend years perfecting their skill, then along comes a snapper who takes a black and white shot of a working class person looking a bit cheesed off. It appears in a Sunday supplement and is called "art". Distinct case of the Emperor's new clothes, if you ask me.'

'You know Brian,' she replied. 'For someone keen on standards and politeness, you can be awfully rude at times,' she said. Her voice had begun in a light-hearted, bantering manner, but a sudden and perhaps involuntary chill descended before she finished the sentence. I took the reproach calmly, but felt shrivelled and unloveable inside.

'To whom?' I asked.

'To modern artists, left-wing people, anyone young.'

'Hmmph.'

We returned to the living room and watched an average-quality television drama based on the music industry, that seemed to involve industrial quantities of Class A drugs, some fast cars, adultery and what was to my ears some quite ghastly music. It was impossible to tell from her expression if Elizabeth was captivated or bored by it, or thinking about other matters entirely, or leaving the show on just to annoy me.

It wasn't late but I said I would go. She accompanied me into her narrow hallway. Then she said: 'What are we doing, exactly, Colin?' she asked as I opened the front door. 'This ... arrangement that we have – we meet regularly but we're not really dating. I, um. Colin, I don't think it really works for me any more. I mean, we're too different; there's your sport, and you are conservative and I'm not, and.... I don't know....'

For a while, she scarcely held my gaze at all as she said this, looking downwards or over my shoulder or about her; then she looked up. As she did so, in the mid-summer dusk, my attention was caught by the bizarre sight of a frog which leapt over the low brick wall of her front garden. The vision, with the setting sun on my head, combined to create a sense of dream.

'There's a frog,' I began. 'How extraordinary!'

She said nothing. All Elizabeth could note was that I avoided eye contact, and coolly said goodbye. Even in my desolation I was mildly relieved, such that, even as I thought I detected a slight hesitation on her part before she softly closed the door with a decisive click, it did not occur to me to check the passage of the closing door with my instep; nor even later to return back down her short front garden path, to knock on her door and beg to talk further. That final sound echoed in my mind as I returned home.

20

Castilian tears

I've always been fond of my neurotic self. We have become friends. It only occasionally gets a telling-off. By middle age, mine had developed a paranoia about lateness; a phobia that I enthusiastically encouraged. If you live on your own, of course, there's no one to rein it in. No one to say: 'Don't be silly'. When it came to flight departures, the fervour to avoid tardiness became accentuated. It meant assuming that if an airline recommends you arrive two hours before departure, it's better to think two and a half or three; I then add another half an hour to be safe. But of course, that assumes the car starts, doesn't break down, and the roads are running well. You could easily add 30 minutes – say 45, to be on the safe side – for each of those eventualities. The M23 can be very busy with Brighton or London traffic in July and August. And then, of course, there's the walk from the long-stay car park. That's another half-hour. This was how I came to be in the Departures lounge, Gatwick, at 10.35 for my 17.45 departure to Madrid. Never mind, I had a good book – several in fact

– and the day's newspaper. There was sure to be somewhere half-decent for lunch.

I had decided on Toledo for a short summer break; that I would finally finish *Don Quijote* in the heart of Castile, and pay a visit to the museum of El Greco. I had caught a sight of the fairy-tale Mediaeval city in a weekend travel supplement and wanted to find a cosy hotel at its heart. I made the booking impulsively, because I was not usually impulsive. I had booked it in the early spring, before I began seeing Elizabeth, so it was always going to be a solo stay; just five days.

In the departure lounge I sat on an improbably small stool at an island coffee bar. The sun was bright through the broad windows, extending nearly a full circle around the lounge, and I sweated uncomfortably, despite my casual clothes (an innovation for the summer) squinting as I read the sports reports and the obituaries – no hard news on holiday; it was a rule.

A young woman carrying a clipboard approached me and told me her life story. She was forthcoming and guileless. I was not sure whether to be touched or humiliated that she saw me as asexual and parental. People had always assumed that I was older than I was; now I really was becoming old. Although in turn, despite her pretty features and short skirt, she provoked not a quiver of desire in me.

'I'm supposed to be selling life assurance,' she said.

'I hope you haven't given up on me because I look too old and ill,' I replied

'No. I'm just not a very good saleswoman.'

'Sales is a very difficult role.'

She accepted my offer of a cappuccino.

'You'd never guess that I have a degree,' she continued. 'I earn £12,000 plus commission, but I don't get many of those, because I'm crap. I was at a school reunion recently, 'cos we'd all turned 30. Samantha, from our class, was always bunking off school, getting into trouble, going to all-night soul discos. Got something like four exams; bad grades. But she married this smart fella. They set up a travel business, now own property across the Mediterranean. Lives in a villa. That's what you get from spending your teenage years shoplifting expensive lipstick and dating guys with nice cars. No justice, is there?' Her elbow was planted on the bar table and her cheek was rested firmly on her clenched left fist, crumpling her facial features to exacerbate their gloomy countenance.

'It's funny the way life turns out,' I replied. 'Still – look at it this way. If she's capable of lifting stuff from stores, maybe she doesn't pay income tax. The property sector is rife with tax evasion. So she could end up in jail some day.'

'Oh, thanks. That's sweet. Just shows – there's always something to hope for, isn't there?' She beamed, stood up in a sprightly fashion and tapped me affectionately on the elbow, as grateful as if my tip for a horse had won her £500. 'Well have a good holiday, sir. What time is your flight?'

'Oh, quarter to six.'

'What?! Oh no, that's a long delay. So you've been here since, like, four in the morning?'

'No, quarter to six this afternoon.'

'Oh. So what are you doing here, then?'

'I like to be in good time.'

Her eyes widened and then she looked to one side, conveying an expression that seemed to say: 'And I thought *I* had problems,' before she sauntered off.

I wandered around the shops, but had nothing really to buy. Then had another coffee. Then wandered around the shops again, before finding a restaurant for lunch. I managed not to fall asleep and miss the flight.

The aircraft lifted me above the clouds and I breathed deeply as my ears popped. I sipped the tepid white wine from the clear plastic cup and let it reach my head quickly. I had money. I was going to Spain. Things could be worse. The warm sun felt fresh and beautiful on my face as I descended from the taxi and strolled into the hotel, climbing nimbly up marble steps adorned by symmetrical palms on either side. Toledo was as beautiful in its miniature but epic grandeur as I had expected.

I was determined to enter a different world. The Test match had started that morning, but I did not seek the score from a radio or a fellow Brit. I would not seek out compatriots at meal times, I resolved. For the first time in my life I did not know the state of play in an England international match. It felt oddly exhilarating; like cutting a cord. It was delightful also to be in a country where I did not know the language. For 20 years I had holidayed in the same small town in the Loire Valley and visited the same wine caves, chateaux and generally staying in one of two or three hotels or in a rented house. Why? Why did I let routine fall upon me like an old cloak? At what point did I decide that life would happen to me and that it was not within my power to take a hold of it in both my hands?

On the first day I spent an hour or two by the riverside, which lies at the foot of the hill on which the central buildings huddle together, marvelling at the pace of fresh water tumbling through an arid landscape, like the breath of life itself. It was good to be thinking of nothing but the sheer miracle of all this. Is this what someone like Elizabeth would call a spiritual moment? Does she experience the same things, and call them differently, or is it a different, higher experience to which I am denied access?

Why was she so obsessed with Brigid? Was it the fact of the relationship, or the way I had treated her? Had it been so very bad? Perhaps some matters were her fault? She hinted that she wanted to end it? No; I tell myself. At least be honest with myself. What happened next, Brian?

I recalled one of just two occasions that I had brought Brigid home; I knew I would have the house to myself.

'Am I going to meet your Ma?' she asked playfully, as she lay naked on the bed, with a comfort and ease that I envied, her head propped up on her hand, looking at me with a face of green eyes and reddened cheeks.

'She's not my mother, she's my aunt; but yes, I guess you will.'

She was reassured by the reply, and rolled onto her back, tucking her hands underneath her head as she closed her eyes, but she should not have been. Only years later did I begin to examine the base motive for my reticence; the discomfort with her accent and background, and my incoherent instinct that, somewhere in the past, Aunt Kath had hinted at anti-Papist prejudices.

'Let's run away together, Brian,' she suggested.

'I'm not very good at running,' I replied, and kissed her.

Perhaps I will gain the chance to live my early life again, perhaps there is another way of looking at my conduct that will prompt another way of feeling about it. It seemed unfair to be imprisoned by time when one has not chosen one's life trajectory. One has choice over the little things in life but not many of the greater ones; though some of the small choices only seemed small at the time.

She did nothing wrong. Nothing. She was sweet. I hurt her because I was a coward; didn't want to show a Catholic girlfriend to my stuck-up Anglican relatives. It was years after that that I first came across the saying 'The greatest coward can hurt the most', and I was puzzled by it and even disagreed; so long did it take me to confront myself with what I had done even though I knew, deep, deep down, that it was as bad a thing as I could do.

What had happened next?

She called me on the phone. I always answered in a conspiratorial whisper, as though we were an adulterous couple. 'Do you want to come with me to London?' she said brightly in her Cork accent. 'I'm going with a friend and her boyfriend. We're going to do the sights and see a show.'

I hesitated, and in that hesitation I felt her illusion collapse. I didn't go with her to London. Indeed, I didn't see her again. Had she really wanted to marry me? Have children? In truth, we did not have much conversation. It may not even have been a happy marriage; and perhaps she is happy now, I reflected. Perhaps she never thinks about me at all.

She left one more message for me, and then sent a note. I did not reply to either.

How wide is the gulf between the best and the worst of us! Godfrey sees me at church every week (well, most weeks), and once I helped him run a charity event over the whole weekend. On another occasion he was being harangued by a most terrible boor in the pub, who was drunk and giving a rude and incoherent lecture on the failings of the Church of England, and I succeeded in distracting the idiot so that he poured out his verbal venom towards me, allowing Godfrey to resume the conversation he sought.

So how do I measure up, as a person? How am I? Spanish has two words that mean 'to be'. One means how we are in the moment; on this day; how we find ourselves. The other means how we are in character, by nature. English is crude;

we use the latter meaning when we mean the former. We stick labels on people. I know how I am but I'm not too sure about who I *am*.

There was a bar in the town that played haunting Brazilian music; like boleros but sexier, by a female singer with a throaty seductive voice. I was reading a book about the conquistadores; about how long ago, before Columbus, Portuguese sailors used to report seeing strange carved wooden statues floating in the ocean when the wind was from the south west; and how the gods of ancient Mexico were white and had beards. Moctezuma thought that Cortes was the returning god Quetzalcoatl.

I also read about the horrors of the age of conquest, which our British history books prefer to call the age of 'exploration'. It included details about the Atlantic slave trade; how much more savage, extensive and long-lasting it was than our school textbooks had sparingly informed us. Rebel slaves would be broken on a wheel, or burned to death. Uprisings were frequent, and were savagely put down. There were dungeons with torture chambers. There were vicious beatings for the most minor misdemeanours. And we were the ones who called ourselves 'civilized'. At least Christians emerged well, for the most part.

I wept silently behind sunglasses, sipping my ice-cold beer in the warm shade, in my embarrassing comfort, watching the torch-like sunshine fill the other half of the cobbled courtyard with a dizzy glow, like many a middle-class tourist on summer vacation, reading of the siege of Stalingrad or the Second Battle of Loos while dabbing themselves with sun cream and tucking in. I was familiar with some of the details of slavery, of course, but not its full duration, nor the extent of the taunting bigotry and calculated sadism. It was the worst crime against humanity until the Nazis and Stalin and Mao, and it lasted much, much longer. It endured for more time than has passed since abolition, blighting the lives of generation after generation. It persisted through every year of the period we like to call the 'Enlightenment'. The transport of slaves was abolished in 1807, the year I had formerly acknowledged as the end of the evil, but slaves were still owned in British Caribbean islands until 1833, and of course the plantations and white rule continued for many decades thereafter. It seems like a long time ago but it really happened. No wonder we Brits go on about the World Wars so much.

I cried real, unwonted tears. I cried for the first time in my life, man or boy, initially with some embarrassment but this disappeared as the wave of grief submerged me. I had not cried at my parents' joint funeral, nor at Aunty Kath's. I had not cried at any heartbreak or setback I had suffered. British men of my generation do not cry. This does not mean that we lack emotion, necessarily; our reserve is intended as respect for others, so as not to impose, nor yield to narcissism. It may not signify repression. If I do not volunteer my feelings, one may always inquire.

But this one day, I cried. I cried too, for my own loneliness, and then with guilt at comparing my comfortable ennui with real suffering. It is not ancient history, I reflected, this momentous crime, now known as *Maafa*, from the Swahili for great tragedy. This was how my great, great, great, great grandfather treated Jeffrey's great, great, great, great grandfather. The legacy has continued well into my lifetime. I recalled a meeting of our two clubs, hosted by our President. It was the early 1980s, and I was a young man. The semi-formal meeting, after our annual match, was to discuss adding a second fixture for the following year, and confirm the timings and arrangements, including for a family barbeque after the game;

confirm likely numbers for the catering, and so on. It was to form part of a week-long cricket festival to celebrate our bicentenary (cricket was invented in the fields of Sussex and Kent, and our club was one of the many ancient ones). All of the older Caribe players, those aged around 35 or above, would seek affirmation from *our* President, the highest-status white man, before accepting that a decision was final; visually awaiting his nod of approval before any decision, almost certainly subconsciously. Even after the matter was settled, some instinctively looked up to him, for confirmation. They all referred to him as Major Charles, the most formal address available (Charles was his surname). By contrast, the younger players and our club members would assume a vote would settle each matter. I recall wondering if I was the only person who noticed.

At the time I was a boy, you had to be white and an amateur to captain the cricket team called the 'West Indies' – islands that are not the 'Indies'; that are called 'West' quite arbitrarily; where most inhabitants descend from Africans, seized by force and chained in the hulls of wooden ships to the slave fields thousands of miles away.

My earliest images of black men were as handsome, brilliant, confident sportsmen: Wes Hall, Mohammad Ali and, above all, Sir Gary Sobers. He played with such élan and genius that I identified with him immediately; much more so than with the more cautious English players, and to such extent that I often supported the West Indies in Test matches. I always sought to play in a similar attacking style. This had been confirmed by an extraordinary incident in a game for the first team that I was playing in when aged around 16 or 17. The opening batsman on our side, early on in an all-day game, began hitting the ball to the boundary. To my astonishment, the captain and some older players thought this was a bad thing! 'He's hitting out too early,' they muttered, and gave him instructions to slow down, shouting from the boundary edge. Needless to say, the guidance confused him and, unsure whether to attack or defend, he was dismissed soon after. We ended up losing by six wickets. I silently coined the term 'hysterical caution' to describe this ridiculous attitude. From that day on, I pretty much ignored the older players, the coaches and their advice. I had my own internalised motto: 'What would Sir Gary do?' which has served me well. It is simplistic to contrast the panache of the liberated man with the overly cautious white administrators, obsessed with borders and control, but perhaps there is a snippet of historical explanation for these apparent cultural differences.

I ordered a light lunch. Vegetarian – after all that reading about torture and the burning of flesh.

The El Greco museum was smaller than I expected: a longish and narrow hall, like the Long Room at Lord's. The paintings were even more angular, startling and original in real life than in reproductions I had seen. There was a well-to-do US family with a personal tour guide. The children were not entirely under control; something I was not entirely comfortable with.

'Hey – these paintings are creepy,' said one.

'Yeah – like a cartoon.'

'Or a horror movie – look at that one, Mom! Like a ghost in Scooby-Doo!'

There was giggling.

'Shh!' said 'Mom', an earnest, white slender figure with long hair, tee-shirt and long shorts, sunglasses pushed up onto her forehead. She was straining to listen to her guide, for whom she had probably paid handsomely.

'....some say El Greco was the first Cubist; moving away from photo-realism to convey the emotion within, illustrating the extreme variability of the human physiognomy…' the art historian opined in her impeccable English with delightful Castilian accent.

I returned to the hotel, both shaken and stirred. Something was going on here.

There is a curious intensity to holiday reading; the opportunity for continuous hours of absorption, without interruption from neighbours or clients, and with no appointments to keep, and perhaps especially when holidaying alone, which I generally did. Next was *Coming up for Air*, which had been on the family bookshelves for years. Aunt Kath was very fond of George Orwell, liking his direct language and confrontation of hypocrisy. The main character, George Bowling, was unnervingly like myself. While I felt nostalgic in the 1990s for the 1930s; for Mr Bowling the ghastliness of commercialism was already rife by the 1930s, prompting warm and nostalgic evocations of unspoilt riversides in the Edwardian age. Then I finished *Don Quijote*; reading of a character of the 1600s nostalgic for the chivalry of the middle ages. There were still Mediterranean galley slaves in the 17th Century. My familiar narratives of decline and decay, and loss of civilization, were undermined. The eras of the renaissance, of baroque art and of Enlightenment were times of unspeakable savagery, hopefully never to be repeated by Europeans.

21

A plea for help

On a typical lonely evening in late summer, there was a knock on the front door. I opened it and there stood Eric Gray, sober and slightly bashful. Can I come in, Brian? He sometimes called me Brian and I always called him Eric, rather than 'Bodger' – the nickname I judged was too pejorative. He was a skilled bricklayer, and his ability at other crafts had reportedly improved over the years, but the nickname stuck. He loved it of course – for the most part.

Our mutual respect stemmed from a game about five years earlier. He was someone very gifted at sport and, though he was a partying lad, with widening girth, who didn't appear to take anything, including his game, terribly seriously, a flash of talent sometimes shone through. In one game, he hit a six with a pull shot from a quick ball scarcely short of a length. After he struck it, the ball never rose more than about eight feet off the ground, yet cleared a long boundary by several yards. I was the non-striking batsman, at the other end, and I scarcely heard the noise of impact, so sweetly did he strike it. His footwork had been too quick to spot. The bowler and I stood motionless for a few seconds, staring at the rapidly disappearing ball in mute astonishment. I strolled down the pitch to him and said: 'I could never have played a shot like that, Eric. You are a genius.' He looked up at me, surprised but clearly elated by my praise, and a little overwhelmed, himself. As a player, the very best shots are guided by pure instinct; the very worst ones, too. There is no conscious decision, never mind premeditation, and you cannot recollect the thought processes of the execution. (And are life decisions also governed by such a process? The very best or the worst made in a moment so fleeting we are without thought; by processes so instinctive that they cannot be reassembled in the memory. The decision is all there is. It is made and it is done).

On another occasion, in the field, he picked the ball up in the covers and, all in the same movement, threw the ball quickly at the stumps, hitting them and running the batsman out by a yard or two. As fielders, we were ecstatic; this kind of intervention turns a match and lifts the whole side.

But this evening I did not meet the usual swaggering, nonchalant chap. He looked worse than dejected; almost broken. His physical appearance was transformed within just a few weeks, from the youthful, good-looking young man with a mane of fair hair to a worried, middle aged fellow. The bruise on his nose from the injury a few weeks earlier was faint but still perceptible. There was a thinning patch on the top of his crown and he displayed the beginnings of a weight problem. I reflected that, while he loved the banter of his team-mates, on some occasions I thought I detected a momentary wince before he laughed at a sarcastic comment about his 'slim' figure, or an inquiry as to whether he was expecting twins. In truth, he was not particularly overweight, just had a paunch developing from too many evenings on beer and fast food, and a striking number of stag parties – he was enormously popular – which tended to last all weekend these days. He was a full ten years younger than me, around mid-30s but in that moment, seemed older.

'You know Julie finally kicked me out a few weeks back,' he told me. I had invited him in and made ourselves a cup of tea. We were sat in the sitting room. 'Well, I think it's for good this time. My back's gone; I've had to give up football, even the pub team. I might even struggle with the cricket next year. But there's more. I can't work on the building projects any more. My Dad keeps saying: work in the office, on the accounts or the administration; there's a job for me there, but I can't.'

'Well, hold on a minute. There are a lot of issues there. Eric – you and Julie are *separated?*'

Eric and Julie had been a golden couple – good looking, successful in the local economy, extroverted and popular. Eric's dad ran a successful building company and Eric helped on the site, destined to inherit a prosperous firm, as the oldest son. Julie worked as a finance manager, was smart and diligent, getting herself promoted even while working part-time. They had two voluble and sweet young children, Jack and Hannah.

I was unexpectedly distraught, given that I was not particularly close to them, at the break-up of such a promising young family. I could not recall an occasion where someone had confided in me on a personal matter, and I wondered why Eric had sought me out. I did not know which issue to discuss first, or in what way, or in how much depth. At that moment I realized that I had not seen Julie at the ground or in the pavilion that summer. In previous years she had been a fairly frequent visitor, sometimes with a pushchair and a toddler in tow.

'I guess I can't blame her,' he said, looking down into his cup, or perhaps straight past it at the floor. 'She warned me last year – cut the drinking and the nights out, even if I don't cut back on the sport I play. I kept meaning to but the lads invite me out, and I don't want to appear to be under the thumb of the missus. But I'm stupid – she means more than they do. And Jack and Hannah as well of course. So, now I'm a lodger in a room – landlady's someone no one knows – but now I'm not even sure I can afford that. I've got to get my life together somehow.'

'So is your dad's firm in trouble?'

'No. No – it's doing well; new contracts.'

'Then why on earth don't you want to keep working there? It's got to be better than being unemployed. You may want to look around but ....'

'No, you don't understand,' he interrupted me. 'It's not that I don't want to – it's that I *can't*.'

'Can't?'

'I can't' .... He paused for a long time, took a huge deep breath, then said: 'read or write. Well, not fluently. I can recognise names and common words, but I get stuck on a lot of sentences.'

'Ah.' I had to think quickly. How would Elizabeth react in this situation? With kindness and offering discretion and help, that's for sure. I had to respond in a way that was helpful, and not patronizing. Fortunately, opening batsmen are trained to think quickly. I managed to say, in what I hoped was a carefree, matter-of-fact way: 'Well, that's not uncommon. You can learn. I can help you if you like.'

'Are you shocked? I feel a bit humiliated.'

'Well not shocked but surprised. You're perfectly intelligent. You're quick-witted, and you're good at mental arithmetic – calculating all those darts finishes or the odds at the bookies.'

'Yea, but that's all in my head. It's writing it down that's the problem. But thanks for calling me intelligent – no one's called me that before.'

'How come you never learned properly?'

'I spent a lot of time playing football, missed lessons; it's quite easy to fake it. I always had a girlfriend to help me with homework. I left school in the April, before the exams. It was obvious that I was either going to play football professionally or work for my dad on the building sites.' He paused, took a deep breath, then added: 'So would you teach me? I'm afraid I can't afford to pay you. I've enrolled on an admin and book-keeping course, starting January. I lied to my dad and told him the September intake was fully booked. I'm on light duties around the sites til then – at least I can drive. So you've got til Christmas to turn me into some civilized, literate and mature human being.'

'Mmm, that's only four months – we might have to settle on one out of the three.'

He gave a sarcastic smile: 'Very funny.'

'Seriously,' I added. 'In principle, I've no problem, it's just – I'm not a teacher.'

'You'll be fine, mate.'

'I'm not sure,' I paused for a moment, then said: 'I know! I know just the person! Elizabeth – you know, she's Shelley's mum; Dale's going out with her. Shelley, that is, not her mum. She's a teacher and is mature and patient and all that. We could ask her!'

Of course, I was in want of a reason to call Elizabeth, though I did not confess that. To my surprise, he looked disappointed at this suggestion; indeed, almost upset.

'You won't do it?' he asked, despairingly.

'Well, in principle; I'm just not sure I have the skills....'

'I don't want to have some headmistressy type, Col. I mean, sorry; Elizabeth's nice but I don't know her. And I don't want anyone else knowing except you. Sorry, I asked…' he began to get up, as if to leave.

'Fine, fine!' I said. 'I was trying to be realistic, that's all. If you're sure you want me to help, then of course, you're on. And I've got a salary and no mortgage, so paying's not an issue. Would give me some company of an evening.'

'Thanks Col. I will owe you big style.'

'Shall we make a start?'

'What now?'

'Why not?'

We began. As he indicated, he was not completely illiterate. He could identify some words and names, and could often grasp the theme of a written passage. It was more the case that he was a slow reader, lacking in confidence, often thwarted by complex sentences and irregular spellings, while his own writing was limited. We made moderate progress, meeting two or three times a week in the late summer and autumn of that year. In many ways, I enjoyed the lessons; they not only gave me company but also a renewed sense of purpose, though the evening that I covered the respective spellings and meanings of 'through', 'thought', 'though', and 'thorough' is not one I would care to repeat. The only time I lost my temper was when he wrote: 'I should of known…'

'But that is so obviously wrong!' I said as I exploded with rage. 'It's should have; should *have!'*

'Then why do people say 'should *of*?' he asked.

'They don't! Well, they shouldn't. Educated people don't. It makes no sense. The word "of" is a preposition! You can't press it into service as an auxiliary verb! It doesn't even begin to make sense! Don't they teach grammar any more? It's a nonsense! It's an absolute fucking scandal!'

Instead of looking abashed, Eric looked rather amused. 'I think that's the first time I've ever heard you swear, Col,' he said, chuckling away. 'This is good. You're teaching me some vocabulary; I'm teaching you some. We're both learning.'

I had to go to the kitchen for a few minutes; put the kettle on and calm down.

22

An end-of-season pub crawl

'Pub crawl!' intoned Derek. 'We chased 260 and got them. That's a club record. Come on! Pub crawl. Starting at the Star. Three line whip.'

It was mid-September, and a Saturday, the penultimate game of the season. The first team were showered and changed and gathered in the pavilion.

'No I've got to go,' I said.

'But you got 67. You're the star! And you haven't bought your jug yet. Come on.'

'Well I can't.'

A group of disapproving stares gathered quickly round me.

'Why not?' asked Dale, angrily.

'Well I can't go to the Star, anyway.'

'Why not? you snob,' he snarled.

Stung, I replied angrily. 'Because I'm barred from The Star.' I emitted this phrase during one of those curious moments of silence that can occur among a constellation of separate conversations. This meant that everyone in the entire pavilion heard me. They turned towards me as one, and most of them, after a pause of disbelief, rather than express shock, collapsed into uncontrolled mirth.

'You can't get barred from The Star. That's where people drink who've been barred from everywhere else. I've heard it all now!' yelped Tony. 'Tell us about when you did time in Wormwood Scrubs!'

More laughter. I was obliged to go. Perhaps, I hoped, the landlord would not recognise me; after all I had only been in there the once. Perhaps he did not really mean it when he said that I would never be welcomed again. I wandered along with the crowd, taking care to loiter near the back. It was late in the season and nearly dark already. The dew was settling in the prim front garden lawns and earthy borders that we walked past on the way to the pub. I felt suddenly cold and depressed as I smelt the dampness.

Tony then turned round to me. 'Are you all right, Col?'

'Yes, fine, thanks,' I replied.

'Not like you to be last in – still, the whole team must owe you loads of drinks. Probably your turn.'

'Yes,' I said simply, as we climbed the two or three steps into the front of the feared establishment. I was near the back of a crowd, hoping to avoid attention, while a few of the others – headed by Derek – approached the bar, and began ordering drinks. Feeling suddenly less nervous, I looked up. It was the same, odious barman, and he looked me in the eye straight away.

'Oi, you!' he said. 'I thought I told you you were barred! Out!'

The entire group was as shocked and silent as if a death sentence had been passed. They actually parted like the wave in the Red Sea as they turned to look at me. I remained mute and motionless, like the others, staring at my accuser from the dock. It was Derek who spoke first. His hour had come. 'Do you mean him?' he asked the landlord, as he pointed to me.

'Yes,' replied the proprietor.

'Do you have any idea who you are talking to?'

'No I don't, and I don't care.'

'Well, I tell you what; we care. No one talks to Col like that. You're barred; this pub is barred by the entire cricket club. We are out of here.'

'Are you going to pay for that pint first?' asked the barman.

Derek picked up his full glass, poured the drink down his throat in two or three gulps, placed the empty vessel ceremoniously on the bar, belched and said 'No,' pointedly, before turning on his heels and leading us out. Everyone cheered. We left.

'Well lads,' I said as we reached the safety of The Swan, choking with fondness for them and worrying that the sight of tears might weaken the masculine solidarity that had arisen so strongly. 'I don't know what to say.'

'What we want to know is,' said Eric. 'What was the story?'

I told them.

'So basically you did nothing wrong or offensive at all?'

'Of course not. We weren't even drunk. We hadn't even had a drink.'

Dale asked: 'He was rude to Elizabeth as well, then?'

'Well yes, he just completely lost it. I mean, it was mostly directed at me, but she was there. His language was foul.'

Dale was furious. 'This guy needs sorting out,' he said, looking very determined.

'Steady now,' said Derek.

'I was just thinking of a little reminder; you know, to treat people with respect.'

I felt emotional and embarrassed at this discussion of

Elizabeth. I told Dale: 'Don't forget she opposes any kind of violence. I don't think she would take kindly to any meted out on her behalf.'

'I know, I know,' he muttered, but still glowered, his black, straight locks falling partly over his face.

'Remember there's a law against grievous bodily harm,' advised Derek.

'I know.'

'And against damaging buildings or cars.'

'I know,' said Dale. 'I'm not a violent man. I don't have a criminal record,' he declared, before quaffing a large slug of beer and adding in a quieter voice: 'Well, not in this country anyway.'

My stock seemed to rise with the other team members upon hearing the tale; for having the notoriety of being barred, but also a certain respect for trying to protect Elizabeth from poor treatment. There were satirical quips also, such as: 'Be careful to treat Col with respect now – he's got a reputation, and a temper.' And: 'If you're ever inside, Col, don't worry – word'll get round that you were barred from The Star and no one will give you any bother.' I was one of the lads, now. I got merrily drunk, properly so, for the first time in years, but I do recall a conversation from the mid-part of the evening, when Dale and Eric drew up a chair each, sat me down and Dale said: 'So – why don't you and Elizabeth get back together?'

This was clearly as long a speech as he could contemplate, so he handed over to Eric, one who talked rather as a bird flaps its wings.

'It's like this, you see Brian,' Eric began. 'We've been thinking, as Dale said, and he's been talking to Elizabeth, who's foster parent to Shelley, who Dale has been dating. Anyway, cut a long story short…'

'You've never done that before,' quipped Dale.

'Well, I'll give it a go,' continued Eric, taking a sharp inward draw on his cigarette, flicking it energetically even though there was scarcely a millimetre of spent ash. My heart had twitched and revolved sharply at the mention of the name Elizabeth.

'Elizabeth is not very happy,' Eric continued. 'Shelley knows it. And if Shelley knows it the world knows it cos, no offence Dale, she doesn't hang about where her opinions are concerned, does she? Anyway Shelley – and she may not be the brightest button in the box, but she's no fool, I can tell you – reckons her mum – Elizabeth to you and me, is not very happy, and she reckons it's an affair of the heart. And I reckon she knows a thing or two about that sort of thing.'

'See what I mean? Never gets to the point.' Dale said to me, jerking his thumb towards Eric, but still abrogating his own responsibility for imparting the apparently momentous intelligence.

'Anyway, as I was saying, Shelley has put two and two together, and reckoned that her Mum is not so well – emotionally. She says her mum has been feeling like this since, well since you and her stopped, well seeing each other.'

I inhaled deeply and sharply. I had been listening intently as they raised their voices above the hubbub of the pub crowd surrounding us at the small, low table. I was moved, puzzled and nervous. 'I doubt that she really wants to see me again,' I said at length.

'Shelley's pretty sure,' said Eric.

'Elizabeth hasn't called me since a few weeks back,' I said.

'Have you called her?'

'Well no, but...'

'Exactly,' he continued. 'You haven't given her the chance.'

'She made it pretty clear...' I protested.

'That was weeks ago,' explained Eric. 'Things change.'

I looked at one and then at the other, becoming more apprehensive still. 'What are you driving at?' I began. 'What are you trying to tell me?'

Eric grinned hugely and said: 'Relax, mate. Relax! We're doing you a favour. Take it from me. Just take our advice, Col.'

I looked at his Coca Cola. I was impressed at his continued resolve, felt mildly guilty that I was drinking beer, and also recognized that he was consciously and soberly offering this friendly advice.

'And what is that?'

'Give Elizabeth a ring. Ask her out for dinner.'

'I don't think she'd be impressed by an obvious move like that.'

'So you admit you'd like her to be – like it's not a case of lack of interest on your part.'

'Well, no, but we're different. It hasn't worked out. Innings over.'

'Well this is the second innings. Learn from what went wrong first time round,' he paused. 'Whatever it was it can't have been that bad. You're good for each other – it's obvious. You've got nothing to lose. Just invite her somewhere nice - you know, the Italian place or that seafood joint or wherever you used to go.'

'What, you mean The Swan?'

'Nah, I mean when you treated her – special occasions.'

'I'm not sure I did, actually,' I confessed.

'What?' Eric raised his eyes with genuine incredulity. 'What were you thinking of? No wonder she got fed up!'

'Well, she's not that sort of woman.'

He clutched his forehead with frustration. 'Brian! I don't believe what I'm hearing! Jeez, you've got a lot to learn.

It's not about whether she's this type or that type. It's making her feel special, that's what. She's still a woman.'

'Well,' I said, wondering if I should be offended at their officiousness, but inwardly feeling rather flattered. 'I'm not sure. When she closed the door it seemed so, well, final.'

'Yea, well that's women, isn't it? Sometimes they mean it. Sometimes it's just a bargaining tool. I suppose we do it too, come to think of it.'

'I suppose I have got a lot to learn,' I acknowledged.

Eric grinned broadly, and slapped me loudly on the shoulder. 'I think he's coming round, Dale, I think we've done well. Good teamwork. Pincer movement. Good cop, bad cop. Go on, mate, get a round in.'

In all the time I had been spending time with Elizabeth, we had rarely, and only nervously, kissed. I thought I was being respectful, especially given her faith, but perhaps I just caused her to feel unattractive. Also, I was fearful of rejection. But this new perspective changed everything. Her response to my tale about Brigid was not her being judgemental. She was jealous.

Clang.

23

You have to be wealthy to bank with Hoares

I was so drunk I slept deeply. My head the next morning was dulled but not too painful. I could remember most of the conversations. And I could remember the advice. Call Elizabeth, ask her out. To dinner? Dinner means bed. But maybe that's what she wants. There was, of course, a cowardly compromise. I could ask for advice on teaching literacy. Yes, that was it. Then dinner. And bed. Maybe. But don't think about that too much.

Eric arrived as usual on the following Monday evening. He looked quite agitated; very nervous but with a hint of joy or fervour, and clutching a few papers.

'I've got an official-looking letter, and a cheque that's made out to me, for rather a lot of money,' he explained. 'I think it must be some scam or some con, or some sales pitch. Can you read it for me? I don't know what to do. It was sent to the family address, marked private and confidential. Julie popped it round. She hadn't opened it, to give her credit.'

'Sure. It would make a good lesson.'

First, I glanced at the cheque. It was from the personal account of a one Iain Lorimer, from the private bank Hoare & Co, which I had heard of, and which I knew served some very wealthy clients. It was made out quite clearly to 'Eric Gray', and the amount, clearly written in digits and in letters, was for £250,000. I said nothing but raised an eyebrow, and unfolded the letter, which ran to two pages, on thick, embossed headed notepaper pertaining to the company 'matrixx' (with a lower case 'm' and double 'x' – I hate such contrived spellings in company brand names, but no matter) and the legend underneath: 'Wealth management for the elite'. The address was St Mary Axe, EC3. The letter-writer was the chief executive. After scanning the pages quickly, I said:

'Eric, I'm just going to read this out to you, and we'll do the lesson later. It is rather important.' I cleared my throat:

'Dear Eric. You may remember me; we were both at Woodside Comprehensive in the 1970s, and we were both in the football team. You were the captain. You may not be aware of this, but you had quite an impact; indeed, you even saved my life one day, which is going to sound terribly melodramatic, but happens to be true. I was having a miserable time at school. Being red-haired and Scottish, and good at lessons marked me out as being different and a geek, and the ribbing I got was unbearable. My parents loved me but they were going through a really rough patch. I think my Mum didn't like the move and wanted to go home to Falkirk. I had actually made a decision to kill myself one evening; had worked out the plans and everything, but first there was a football match to play. You may be thinking: why I on earth would I bother playing the game if I was going to commit suicide a couple of hours later? I think it had something to do with wanting to be active for a few hours until it was dark. Plus, it was a quarter final, and I couldn't see you a player short.

'Anyway, in the warm-up a couple of the lads were having a go at me, as usual. I can't remember the insults, or what they said, I just recall being on the receiving end of all this venom and spite, without having done anything or knowing why. At that precise moment, I was probably the most miserable specimen in the whole world, and I felt relief that it was all going to be over in a few hours. After a minute or two of this, you came over. "Oh, God," I thought, "Now the skipper's going to join in." But instead, you gave the other two a rollicking! I think the gist was: "Back off, we're all on the same team – I want you lot solid at the back. This is a cup tie. Any more crap like that and you're dropped for the next game." They shut up and walked away. Then you gave me a wink, tapped me on the shoulder and said: "Have a great game Iain, you're a better player than those wankers anyway." Well, we won, as you may recall. In fact, we won the cup that year. You didn't just do the right thing – you were incredibly brave. Those kids were the roughest in the year, well capable of beating me up – or you for that matter – but you faced them down. It remains the most impressive bit of leadership I have ever witnessed.

'It wasn't just that incident; over the next year or two, thanks to your support and your example, I began to grow in confidence. I felt part of a team for the first time. Your example of leadership was an inspiration; the way you maintained discipline and encouraged everyone, and insisted that we never gave up. Do you remember the match where we were 3-0 down at half time and ended up with a draw? You personally rallied everyone and scored the equalising goal.

'Since I started my own company six years ago, your example has helped me lead a team: how you can hold people to account for their performance, but always encourage them to do better and make them feel inspired and good about themselves. Without doubt that has helped me build my business, as well as keep me out of the tribunals. I think that without you as a role model I would have been too introverted, or too severe, as a boss, or both, or never had the confidence to start a business in the first place. I think about you every time I chair a meeting or hold a performance review. I ask myself: How would Eric have handled this?

'Now that I have become successful, I want you to accept this gift as a token of my enormous gratitude, and to assure you that I will always remember and value your immense contribution in my life – since you saved it that day.

'Fondly, and with thanks. Yours. Iain Lorimer.'

There was a long silence, impossible to interpret. Eric didn't look at me, but rather over my shoulder. At last he said: 'That's really what it says?'

'No, I just made it up. Of course that's what it says! You must have been quite an inspiration to him!'

'Well, I remember Iain, yeah. Red-head. Wasn't in my class, he was in the top group – a bit of a maths whizz, I think. But a good footballer – a better player than he thought he was. Skinny but strong in the tackle, and when he passed the ball he pinged it right into my feet. Then, in the final, I think, he got possession in a bit of space and put in a perfect through ball to set up the winning goal. I think he was a bit more popular after that. But I can't remember that bit where I pulled the bullies off of 'im. Can't remember that at all. But if I did it, I just saw it as my job as captain – you know, keep the troops together, stop any squabbling in the ranks.'

There was a long silence. Then he said: 'So can I accept it?'

he began to smile a little, though nervously. 'I'm still not sure I should. It doesn't feel right. I can't even remember that incident.'

'Well, it does sound genuine,' I replied. 'But with such a large sum of money, in my experience as a lawyer, there just may be complications. Invisible strings attached. Iain does include the contact details of his lawyer, as a postscript. So what I propose is that I represent you – no fee; as a favour.'

'Lawyers? Why do lawyers have to get involved?'

'In a situation like this, sometimes lawyers have to get involved in order to make sure that lawyers don't end up getting involved.'

'Well, that doesn't make any sense at all.'

'What I mean is: a bit of digging might prevent an unwanted complication.'

'Such as?'

'Accepting such a large sum could be interpreted as entering a de facto contract, with conditions attached or implied; there may be an ex-wife, or soon-to-be ex-wife with children and a claim on a share of this amount who starts giving you grief. Pure speculation, but it might just be worth your while to check things out and give you peace of mind. It appears to be most genuine and uncomplicated, but we could maybe just find out a bit more, to put your mind at rest. If there's any ambiguity on the claim, I could sort that out for you. Don't worry, I'll do it all *pro bono*.'

'What?'

'Pro bono.' I said, clearly.

He paused, and looked puzzled. 'Bono? What does he have to do with it? I never liked U2. Simple Minds are all right.'

'What are you talking about?' I asked.

'What are *you* talking about?'

'The arrangements for representing you.'

'Oh. Are you? Well, it's good of you Col.'

'No problem.'

'Will I have to pay?'

'No! Of course not. That's what I was trying to explain.'

'OK! OK! Why didn't you just say so?' he asked. Then added: 'And you reckon he's pretty rich?'

'You have to be wealthy to bank with Hoares.'

'You *what!?*' he exclaimed, in a raised voice.

'No, no – Hoare & Co. H-O-A-R-E, not W-H-O-R… oh, wait a minute, you can't spell, can you? Well, it's an unfortunate company name but a very highly respected company – as much as say Sotheby's or Rolls Royce. Just take it from me that he is at least fairly wealthy and very possibly has more money than the government. But I'll find out.'

'Thanks Brian. I owe you.'

'No you don't.'

I called the lawyers the next morning. They were charming, friendly. They were also keen to see me promptly, which was either a very good sign or a very bad one, and we arranged a meeting for the next day. It occurred to me that most of my suits were a little tweedy and shabby, and the one relatively fashionable one had been worn and dry-cleaned quite heavily over the past year or two. I didn't want to come across as the bumbling country solicitor. I had savings, so I decided to treat myself; took the afternoon off and drove to a department store in Guildford. I was lucky and had a lovely assistant who guided me to the smartest suit that would not be out of place on the (slightly) portly figure of a middle aged man. I bought some new shirts, ties and cuff links for good measure, and a new pair of shoes, spending more on clothes that afternoon than I had in the previous five years.

The London offices of Reaney & Jones solicitors were on

Queen Victoria Street. I took the train to London Blackfriars and walked from there. The building was not particularly high-rise, but modern and chic, with glass elevators and spacious offices. I met a senior partner, who spoke firmly and quickly, but she was also friendly and keen to put me at my ease. She led me into her roomy office on the third floor, just high enough for a view over the River Thames. We sat on opposite sides of a huge glass desk, on square-backed swivel chairs with black leather fittings.

I began: 'My client is very grateful but also surprised to hear from your client after so many years. He is also very conscientious, and wanted me to check a few things before accepting this generous gift.'

'That's perfectly understandable, and thanks for coming to see us at short notice,' she said. She was about my age; suited and immaculately coiffured, and looked vaguely familiar. After a while I recalled. We were at law school together. Her business card said 'Karen Harvey', and the memories came back: top of the class, a real high-flier, sometimes dubbed 'Future PM' by way of nickname. It was quite clear that she did not remember me.

'What would you like to know?' she asked.

'Well, just some reassurance … um clarification that this is an uncomplicated gift, not an implied contract.'

'Absolutely. I can assure you of that.'

'And that there aren't … competing claims on the sum. Perhaps an ex-wife….'

'I can assure you of that. Absolutely.'

'And, not really a legal matter; but off the record: this is not a significant sum for your client?'

She almost broke into a smile. 'Off the record, my client spent more last month on a birthday party for his partner. It was a concert in the south of France. Rod Stewart was on the bill – his partner wanted to duet with him.'

'Ah.' Even I had heard of Rod Stewart. 'So, he has a partner? Is she aware …'

'Well, off the record *he,*' she said with exaggerated emphasis, 'is successful and wealthy in his own right. He is also an established pop star who protects his privacy.'

She looked me directly in the eye, scrutinising my face for the merest hint of disapproval. Smart, cosmopolitan modern, she had no discomfort at a homosexual relationship and could not be certain of the reaction in a provincial lawyer of pre-war dress and manners. For myself, the instinctive difficulty a Christian of my generation would have with the subject was tempered by an acute respect for privacy and a liberal disposition. It was clear to me that Benjamin Brittan and Peter Pears had been lovers, and there was nothing in the gospels on the subject at all, something the conservatives keep quiet about.

'Ah. I see.' I gave a nod of approval that must have been convincing, as she seemed to warm to me a little.

'Large female fan base,' she informed me, conspiratorially and with a small but unmistakeable twinkle in her eye, and a tiny involuntary shudder, betraying that she herself formed part of said demographic.

'Right,' I replied. 'So not likely to come down to mid-Sussex in pursuit of a share of what is, for him, a relatively small sum of money, that he doesn't have a claim on anyway and probably doesn't even know about, risking publicity.'

'Indeed.'

'It has been a pleasure doing business with you.' We stood to shake hands.

'Can I just add, Mr Clarke?' she said. 'This is an absolutely genuine, uncomplicated and heartfelt gesture, and I hope it makes a difference to your client's quality of life. My client speaks most highly, almost reverently, of your client, and feels a pressing need to reward and recognize him; as though every day he lives is a gift from him. I proposed to him that he might want to draft a short contract, including a clause preventing your client from future requests for financial assistance, but he absolutely refused. I have never seen him so emotional about any matter. He even,' she hesitated for a moment, then began again. 'He referred to your client as having been his saviour; his *guardian angel*. That was the actual term used. I felt slightly embarrassed but he was not – not a bit of it. I believe he wrote a personal note to your client, setting out his reasons. When I told him this morning I was meeting you he made a point of saying that if there's anything else he could do for your client – I assume he means non-financial, and reasonable requests – he can get in touch.'

She smiled and wrinkled her nose a little, in a gesture of complicity between us that said 'Ah, youngsters!'

I could not, of course, admit to her that Eric had been unable to read the letter, and had handed it to me to do so for him. Instead, I said: 'If my client does approach your client with future requests, be sure to get in touch with me, and I'll have a word. But I rather doubt it. He's a good man. Not perfect at all, but honourable in the things that matter.'

I was back on the train within an hour of arriving. I sat back in my seat, chuckling at the thought of Eric – our Bodger; team clown and champion drinker – being the guardian angel of a king of capitalism with more money than Rockefeller. Mysterious ways, indeed. I couldn't wait to tell Elizabeth – the only person I knew who believed in guardian angels – about this! Then a renewed wave of anxiety spread over me as I worried over whether this would ever be possible. While I remained uncertain of my chance of a rapprochement with Elizabeth, an idea for reconciling Eric and Julie had begun to take shape.

24

An early finish

I was mildly troubled, worrying about a slight, though to my mind harmless, breach of confidentiality that I was planning. Once home, I set about my simple task. I was someone who neatly filed back issues of *The Telegraph*, and I recalled a Diary item from a couple of weeks earlier that wrote of a lavish celebrity party in a venue close to Antibes. I found the desired item with no difficulty, and learned that it was for the occasion of the birthday of a famous singer, one Jed Collins. I hadn't heard of him. An accompanying picture showed a white man with jet black hair, a handsome face, dimpled chin and winning smile. The writer gushed. She also mentioned that he had been joined on stage by Rod Stewart. The report made no reference to the organizer and benefactor of the event, giving the impression that it was the singer himself.

I was due at Eric's the next day. He was at the family home, looking after Hannah and Jack while Julie was out with her girlfriends. At least, Eric and I hoped she was with friends. The children were in bed by the time I arrived and I briefed

Eric about my meeting at the law firm. He made me a cup of tea. No champagne, no wine, no beer. Not for a few weeks or even months, he promised. He was trembling with nerves; clearly delighted but unsure how to express his bewilderment, gratitude and excitement.

'Still feel like I don't deserve it.'

'On the contrary, it sounds as though you're due some good luck. You saved a young boy's life. You were brave. You did the right thing – it hardly matters that you can't remember it. He wants to thank you, and to help you now he's able.'

We began the lesson. During his comfort break I got up to scan the racks of records and CDs. They were in strict alphabetical order – this would be the work of Julie, the organised finance manager. There was a large Phil Collins section – odd, I thought; the nickname 'Sticks' of his namesake in our cricket team was reportedly due to the famous Phil Collins being a drummer – but in these albums he appeared to be a singer. Perhaps there were two Phil Collinses in the world of pop and rock, I reflected. Next to them were a half a dozen CDs credited to young Jed. *My Guardian Angel*; *Jed Collins and Friends Sing Jazz*, *Just for You* and a few others. His style seemed quite retro – more Dean Martin than rock n roll. I didn't get the feeling that these recordings belonged to Eric.

I was seated again when he returned.

'Is the lesson over?' he asked.

'I guess, yes, we've covered a lot.'

He started to become very twitchy, fiddling with and looking at his watch. 'Do you really think she's with girlfriends?'

'Eric, don't torture yourself. She'll be back soon.'

'Yeah of course. Stop worrying,' he told himself, in the most anxious voice imaginable. 'What's the time?'

'It's only 10.30,' I said.

'Yea, of course. Another cuppa?'

'Sure.'

He returned with the cups. 'What's the time now?'

'About five minutes after the last time you asked. 10.35.'

'Of course, sorry.' Long silence. 'I bet she's with *him*.'

'Who?'

'I haven't told you the worst part.'

'Oh.'

'It was about, oh, early August. I came home early from cricket 'cos we won easy. Do you remember? Nine wicket win at that club in Crawley. We were only chasing 75. So I gets home. Strange car in the drive. I let myself in, could hear noises upstairs and – well you've guessed it. She was in our bed, with this…this man. They were, well naked, or nearly so. Of course I pissed him off out of the house. Scared him, I think. She was crying. It was horrible. But then, instead of apologizing, like I expected, you know, begging for forgiveness, she tore into me. She said I'd been absent, I'd been drunk I was the missing Dad, and anyway how I'd shagged Sally the barmaid from the pub. But still. In our house.'

'Did you sleep with Sally?'

'What? No, well yes, well once. We were pissed and her flat is right by the pub. But *Julie*. In our house. In our bed. He.... she... I was nearly sick. In fact, I think I was sick on the drive. I got in the car and drove about 100 miles, found a hotel. Stayed there a couple of days. Didn't call.' Long pause. 'You won't tell the lads will you?'

'What, that you slept with Sally?'

'No!!' he said with exasperation. 'I don't mind them knowing that. Please don't tell them that Julie was seeing someone. Is seeing someone. Maybe. I don't want them saying bad things about her; plus it's a humiliation for me. You're the only person I've told. *Will* ever tell.'

'Of course. I'm used to confidentiality – it's part of my work. You have my word.'

'I never thought she'd cheat on me. For days, I was mad with her: that she could even think of sleeping with someone else just 'cos I'd turned 30 and put on a bit of weight. Never thought she was that shallow. Then I thought completely the other way around: maybe it's all been my fault. I'd taken her for granted; hadn't been there enough. You know, gone out with the lads too much. I mean, the sport: well, she knew I played a lot of sport. She liked that. I could have been a professional footballer. She'd have liked that. Especially the money, these days. It could all have been different.'

There was a long pause. 'You know I was on the books at Crystal Palace, don't you? When I was 15.'

'I didn't – but it doesn't surprise me. You're a natural sportsman.'

'I captained the under-15s against Fulham. At Selhurst Park, under the floodlights. My Dad promised he'd get there. Promised. Like all his bloody promises. Two minutes before the game, there's my mum, in the stands, just above the dug-out. On her own. She talks to me after the game and it's all like: "Oh your Dad wanted to come but his most important client had an emergency." Only, days later, I heard he'd been seen coming out of a restaurant with his PA, that horrible flashy bird called Sharon. Some bloody emergency. He was probably doing her, wasn't he? Anyway, no excuses, but I had a bad match. Nerves got to me. Was off the pace. Let the ball under my feet once, made a couple of rash challenges, got yellow-carded. Had a go at the referee. Those things get noticed. The scouts and the coaches were there. Even the first team manager. Just not my dad. I played a couple more times but by then I was already starting to go down the pub and enjoy it. I don't think my dad turned up for a single bloody game I was playing in. Not even at school. And he'd always belittle the trophies and awards I got. Always.'

An actual tear appeared on Eric's cheek, and the rims of his eyes were bright crimson. Astonishingly, he was not in the least embarrassed, and instead seemed in possession of a quite distant look. Would it be patronising to offer him a handkerchief? I offered biscuits instead. He took one, munching slowly, oblivious to the few crumbs that cascaded off his chin and into his cup and his lap.

'Have you ever played in front of a crowd, Col, heard the cheer or the round of applause?'

'Not really,' I replied. 'Well, there were a couple of thousand at Hove when I played for the county, but I was out second ball so never got an ovation, exactly.'

'I played a couple of seasons non-league, and one year we got to the FA Cup First Round against a Fourth Division club. We had maybe 1,500, 2,000 – sell-out, anyway. I scored. Just a tap-in, but they all count. Crowd went crazy.' There was a flicker of a smile. 'Just a couple of thousand. But imagine it was 60,000, or 80,000.... Just imagine. Makes you shiver, don't it?'

We shared a long silence at the thought.

'Still,' he said, shaking himself out of his reverie. 'When you're young you think sport's more important than marriage. Takes something like all this happening to make you think again. Do you think Julie will want me back now?'

'Probably not a good idea if money is the only reason. It might be better to buy a nice semi-detached house for yourself with rooms for the kids, so they can visit and stay with you. Decorate it nicely. Then take it from there. See how your relationship with Julie changes. Do not buy a new car.

Do not go on any expensive holidays. Start a savings fund for Jack and Hannah's college expenses. Start to be a better Dad to them than your's was to you. That's your job now.'

'Good advice.'

'And Eric?'

'Yes?'

'If you piss this any of this money up the wall I will personally break both your legs and make it look like an accident. You've been given a chance to have another start at adult life and it's probably the last one you'll get.'

'Understood, captain.'

At that moment, we heard the sound of a key in the front door. Eric jumped up, almost crying with relief. Julie walked in, calm and relatively sober. He was warm, welcoming, effusive. She was friendlier than I expected, though a little cool towards him; respectful to me as she always was. She strongly approved of the lessons. I suspected that the principal reason was my insistence on Eric's sobriety for the duration, but no matter. She was the only one to know about them, in addition to Eric and myself. Perhaps Julie had just been with a couple of girlfriends, sipping wine and talking about their kids and what was in the charts. She didn't know about the money yet.

25

Christianity is not some sort of religion

We met in a café, not a pub. I asked after Shelley. We circled a few subjects. It wasn't as easy as I had expected. After a while, she held eye contact with me for the first time. It was most penetrative. Eye contact can be more intimate than touch. She was searching; yearning; loving and wary all at the same time. 'So, Colin, how are you?'

'Actually, I'm fine. How are you?'

'Fine.'

But then there was another pause which, for me at least was awkward. I sought to keep to safe subjects. 'How's your aunt?' I inquired, in a compassionate tone.

'Still dead,' she replied.

'Oh.' Had she told me? She must have told me. 'Well, I knew it was serious,' I added, unhelpfully. 'My capacity for verbal and social ineptitude has not been cured over the summer, you'll see.'

She smiled. 'Don't worry Colin, it's one of the things I like about you.'

She looked rather relaxed and a little tanned. She seemed to have had a good summer, which made me feel both pleased and jealous. But listen again, I told myself: she said she liked me. It took a minute or two for the warm glow of this phrase to feed all the way through my body. 'Have you been on holiday?' I asked.

'Yes, we went to northern Spain.'

'We?' I asked, alarmed, and considerably more jealous.

'Some friends and I went to the Picos de Europa in August to do some hill walking.'

'I went to Spain too – to Toledo. About the same time.'

'Did you go walking?'

'Good Lord, no. In that heat? No, I went to the El Greco museum, ate good food and drank Rioja or cold beer, like a civilized person. Read a lot of books.'

'The mountains were wonderful!' she said. 'Although a couple of my colleagues were even more keen on the extreme hike than me, so I might have snuck off to Toledo for lunch with you had I known! And had more time to read.'

'That would have been nice.'

'What did you read?' she asked.

'A most extraordinary collection – just thrown together, but with some powerful common themes. My literary angel assembled a most astonishing mini-library. Well, among others, *Coming up for Air* by George Orwell, and *Don Quijote*. Turns out, I didn't invent nostalgia after all. It's been around for a very long time.'

She smiled. I told her about the shocking historical details of the slave trade, most of which she was already familiar with. 'So you've turned politically correct in your old age?' she asked, teasingly.

'Absolutely not!' I replied. 'My patriotism was challenged,

but not my faith. Slavery was abolished by Christians in the 19th Century, only to be reintroduced by atheist dictatorships in the 20th.'

'Interesting take,' she replied.

'You disagree?'

'No. Well, it's a valid narrative, though there are always several. I'm becoming rather less strident myself, as it happens. To tell you the truth, a couple of my colleagues on the walking holiday became a bit tiresome; going on about some cause or other, not tolerating debate, not acknowledging an alternative point of view. I set out more or less agreeing with them, but became less sympathetic as they went on. I'd have gladly joined you for a bottle of Rioja to talk about England's chances in the Test match. And I did rather warm to your idea of Groucho Marx chairing an editorial committee for a new edition of the Bible.'

'Oh, not *chairing* the committee,' I protested. 'Be realistic.'

'Still a cool idea. You know, the problem with Christianity is that people for or against it just treat like some sort of religion.'

I looked at her with a steady gaze. 'You've lost me again.'

She beamed, and said nothing.

When I told her about Eric, she started to be intrigued. She had taught adults with literacy problems, and offered me to loan some teaching materials.

'We have to get Julie and him back together,' I said.

'Mmm. Don't go "saving",' she advised.

'What?'

'You're trying to be a rescuer. Your initiative is wonderful, but I'd be careful about either intervening too much, or expecting things to go to a script. Events rarely do.'

'Oh. Don't you think I should try to reunite a young married couple with two children, who still care about each other?'

'I think they're grown-ups, and what you're doing with Eric will help his self-confidence, help him grow up and find his own way back to her, if he wants to. And if she will have him back.'

'I do have a plan for the cricket club do,' I explained. 'Have you heard of this singer Jed Collins?'

'Yes, of course; he's a superstar.'

'Really?'

'An absolute dish.' She shivered just as Karen Harvey had done. Whatever magnetism this dashing young singer had could penetrate the most mature and educated of his clearly immense female fan base. The boy from Falkirk had married well. He had also broken the hearts of most of the female population of the western world, even though they were yet to realise. 'I especially love that song *My Guardian Angel* – bit sentimental, but beautifully sung. He always says it's about someone special. I wonder who she is.'

'Yes. I wonder. Funny how people who aren't religious still get mushy over angels.'

'Indeed. Anyway, why are you asking?' she said.

'If I were to call in a huge favour, maybe I could get him to sing at the club's Christmas do. I've found out that Julie is a fan.'

She laughed out loud. 'Good luck with that!'

I was rather cross at this response, but her familiarity with me was encouraging. 'So are we back together?' I asked, nervously.

'I'm not sure if we were ever together,' she replied.

'Would you come to the cricket club Christmas do I'm planning?'

'Of course,' she replied.

'And not only because Jed Collins is going to be singing there. At least I hope he is. Confidentially, of course.'

'Thank you, Colin. It would be lovely.' She picked up my hand and gave it a squeeze.

'And, um before that, would you come out for dinner one evening?'

'Of course.'

'It's a date, then.'

'About bloody time,' she replied. Dale, Shelley and Eric were spot on, then.

26

Events management

The ringing tone sounded just once before the efficient personal assistant answered. 'Reaney & Jones, Karen Harvey's line.'

'It's Brian Clarke here. Could I speak to Karen Harvey?'

'What's it regarding?'

'It's to do with Iain Lorimer.'

'I'll put you right through.'

Greetings were brief. She was busy and I came quite directly to the point. 'When we met you mentioned that Mr Lorimer was keen to help my client in non-financial ways.'

'Yeeees,' she said carefully. Guarded. That was to be expected.

'Please don't worry. It's just an idea I'd like you to run by you.'

It required a face-to-face meeting. A couple of days later I took the train to Blackfriars once more. To my astonishment, Iain Lorimer himself was there: active and fidgety; effusive and highly communicative. He had a wide face, high cheek bones and a slightly startled expression that appeared to be permanent. The reddish hair was just beginning to recede above the forehead. Piercing blue eyes gave off a frightening intelligence. He seemed lean and trim – clearly still active in sport of some kind. He was terribly friendly to me, and when I related to him – in the broadest of outlines – some of Eric's recent travails he become most emotional, and appreciative to my fatherly concern. I did not allude to his problems with literacy, rather putting the emphasis on help with sorting out his financial affairs and accommodation.

There was also a very chic and heavily made-up woman, who stayed quiet and was introduced to me as Amy, Jed Collins' PR adviser.

I didn't get into trouble for having worked out who Iain's partner was, and I was hoping Karen hadn't either, for having given the most oblique clue. It was quite clear that Iain intervened directly, and was doing his best to ensure that my plans worked out, for the sake of Eric. There was a list of stipulations, however. A long list. Mostly to do with security and privacy. I had to sign a contract. There was to be media activity, but only after the event, Amy informed us. The singer had attracted controversy recently; on one occasion over a drunken row with a press photographer in a London night-club, and on another over a legal but rather zealous tax minimisation scheme that his financial advisers had dreamt up. Some favourable coverage of his guest appearance at an 'ordinary' fan's birthday party could make him more likeable again. He had a chance of the Christmas Number 1 that year, but had lost a little goodwill in the UK. Amy talked in terms of 'lines' and 'angles' to take with media outlets, and 'visuals' to pursue, discussing the singer as though he were a consumer product – which, from her professional point of view, in a sense he was. A professional photographer was to pose as one of the guests, and a shot of Jed Collins with Julie was to be arranged.

Amy was to offer a friendly journalist in the tabloid newspapers an exclusive arrangement for the photo-story. Quotes, including one from me anonymously as a friend of the 'fan' were to be drafted in advance. I felt a little uneasy at the simplification of the truth that the 'line' involved – that this guest appearance was a simple treat by a man to surprise his wife on her birthday – but it was close enough to the real version to satisfy me. By a fortunate coincidence, Julie's birthday was in late November.

After terms were agreed, Karen spoke up: 'There is one final requirement that I would like to insist upon, from my perspective, more than from Mr Lorimer's.'

Her client looked up sharply, but curious and not hostile.

'Yes, what is that?' I asked.

'Can I attend too?'

We all laughed – well, except the stern PR lady, who appeared mildly cross, looked down and scribbled a few notes on her pad.

The next challenge, however, was to ensure that Julie actually turned up. The idea, which I had already lined up with Derek, was to have a bigger do than usual for the cricket club's post-season party, with a live band and singer. The problem, naturally, was that Julie would probably prefer to do an unpaid shift at work or sit in the stocks on the village green for an hour than have anything to do with Eric or any of his sporting buddies. Eric himself had little or no leverage, for obvious reasons. We had to turn to her best friend Nisha. Fortunately she and Craig were still dating, and getting along well. The four of us met in The Swan.

'You have to get her to come to our cricket club annual dinner,' I explained. 'Eric and I are arranging a special entertainment for her birthday.'

'Well, I'll try,' said Nisha. 'Sell it to me.'

'Well, you can't tell her in advance, as it's a surprise, but I've booked Jed Collins,' I replied, playing my trump card straight away.

She laughed; not the response I was expecting. 'So you've got some tribute act. I suppose we could go see him – check if he's any good.'

'No,' I said, firmly and mildly annoyed. 'I've got the real Jed Collins.'

'Right, so you've got the "real" Jed Collins,' – she made air quote gestures with both forefingers – 'Turning up for the cricket club Christmas do. I guess Elvis is still alive and going to join him for the encore. So, I'm not allowed to tell her about this improbable event – yet still persuade her to come along.'

'Make something up,' suggested Eric. 'Women are good at that.'

'Make up what? I suppose I could say I've organized something special – us and the girls, for her birthday.' She looked at me. 'This guy had better be good.'

'Well, he's not really my cup of tea, but he's sold millions of records around the world, apparently, and Julie's a fan,' I replied, still rather cross.

She gave me a long, steady look. 'You're serious?' she asked. She had still been thinking in terms of a tribute act. My ignorance of pop and rock music was legendary, so her scepticism was understandable. I looked her straight in the eye. 'I'm serious.'

'How did this come about?'

'I can't give details. It's confidential.'

Her look became more sceptical again. Craig chipped in on my behalf: 'Nisha – Col's a Christian and a top lawyer. He wouldn't make stuff up or get it wrong.'

'You've got to tell me something more Col, about how it came about,' she asked me.

'Well, without giving any names or specific details, let me just say that I know his partner's lawyer and I was able to call in a few favours.'

'His *partner*??!!' she asked, wide-eyed with excitement. 'I knew it! I knew he was dating! What's she like? She must be beautiful. Is she blonde? Is she Indian – a Bollywood beauty? Am I close?'

'Not really,' I replied.

'Come on, you must give us a clue.'

'I can't – I'd get sued.'

'Oh, don't be so melodramatic.'

'I'm not. I've signed a contract. I really would be sued. Clause 4.1.'

'I bet she's married,' said Nisha. 'That's it! He's dating a famous Hollywood actress who's married to someone else, equally famous. That explains why he's so secretive!'

'No hints,' I said. 'No details. Just get Julie there, please.'

'OK, you've got yourself a deal: I'll make sure she gets there. You make sure the real Jed Collins turns up. So glad I've worked it out,' she said, rather smugly. 'Of course, if he's looking for a single lady, I'll be there.'

'Hey – you're not single,' said Craig.

'We're not engaged, are we?' she replied sharply.

'So you'd dump me for this drippy singer, would you?'

'Like a shot – but don't take it personally. You could date Sharon Stone.'

'OK. Suit yourself,' said Craig grumpily. 'I bet he's gay anyway.'

She pulled a face at him. At this point I buried my face in my pint of beer. The most momentary eye contact with Craig at that point and the truth would be out.

27

Dinner date

The dinner – the 'date' – finally took place. I dressed in a suit; Elizabeth in her best posh frock, and, quite unexpectedly, some make-up. 'Shelley showed me how to apply it,' she explained, beaming.

'You've spent some money on yourself,' I said, approvingly.

'You've smartened up a little too – lost some weight, I think.'

'I have indeed. All this extra tutoring, sober evenings and early nights; helping young Eric stay on the wagon. I have to set an example.'

'Why did it take you so long to ask me out properly?'

'It was fear of rejection. The last time I asked someone out – a lawyer at another firm, but not in a role that was ever likely to mean we'd be up against each other, she said no so derisively it rather took the wind out of my sails. So I hadn't had the confidence since.'

'When was that?'

'Oh, quite recently. About six years ago.'

'Six *years*?'

'Yes.' There was a silence. I added: 'It can be quite lonely, living on your own; desperately lonely, some evenings, even when you have plenty of friends. Someone of my background and generation doesn't regard sexual gratification as an entitlement, like the hippies or many youngsters today; but to live without a caress, or a tender word, or a comforting hug; without someone to fix you a cup of tea and ask about your day; that's very hard. And it's difficult to admit being lonely, because to do so just repels people even more.'

There was a long silence. I hadn't thought I was feeling particularly sorry for myself, but she picked up my hand and held it firmly for several minutes. After dinner, in the street, finally, then, we did kiss. It was wonderful.

'So why did you hardly ever kiss me during all the time we were seeing each other over the summer?'

'*I* kiss *you*? What is this, the 19th Century?' I asked. 'What happened to your principles of equality?'

'I leaned in a couple of times,' she protested.

'Did you? How?'

'Like this.' She leaned forwards, eyes closed; slight pucker.

'You just look like you're falling over. I probably thought you were drunk.'

'Well, there are no evening classes for 42-year-old spinsters on how to get kissed. Birds do it, bees do it, teenagers know how; it's just middle-aged Christians who take themselves too seriously who need specialist help.'

'So, what about our political differences?'

'Well Colin. We often have different perspectives, but we have the same values.'

'Do we?'

'Yes.'

'Well if you say so, that's settled then,' I replied. 'Just one thing: do we have to determine whether you call me Brian or Colin?'

'Well, I would have thought it's quite straightforward. I shall call you Colin if I am pleased with you, and Brian if I am rather cross.'

'We should do a weekly tally – see which you use more.'

'What an excellent idea.'

28

The stage is set, the mics are on

On the evening of the party, I arrived early. I had already attended the venue in the afternoon with a couple of Jed Collins' people to set things up. The hotel we had chosen had a proper venue for small or medium-sized concerts; a discreet rear entrance, and changing facilities. He was to arrive at some point in the early evening. One of his minders would come through to the bar to let me know. The idea was: a buffet from 7.30 til 8.30, then a few warm-up numbers by the band, before the headline act took to the stage between 9 and half past. At that point, some of his security folk, with assistance from hotel staff, would move to the front of house to seal the entrances, just in case word had got out around the town and a crowd were building up outside.

It was billed as a fund-raising concert for the cricket club. As a backing band, I had put forward Graham's jazz quintet. Rather to my surprise, Jed Collins' people accepted this, after checking the musicians' résumés. It would be more discreet to have a local group and their standard was very high, with members having played at Ronnie Scott's and the like. Subject to strict confidentiality agreements – which actually had to be signed and witnessed – the five of them agreed, and spent a couple of weeks learning a selection of the star's hits.

Derek had offered to give a welcoming speech on behalf of the club, and summarize the main achievements of the past year and plans for the coming year, but after some deliberation the committee concluded that this would necessitate a considerable discount to the pricey charge of £15. The Treasurer argued most strongly on the point, and won the day. No speeches.

By 7.15, I was smartened up, greeting the first few arrivals, inwardly nervous but trying to project calmness. Eric was also early, clutching his Coca Cola with lemon and ice. I admired his continued self-will, and felt mildly guilty at sipping from a gin and tonic, though relieved that it kept the jitters at bay. If anyone had offered me a cigarette at that point, I would have taken it. Graham joined us, totally free of nerves, as super-intelligent folk often are, and enjoyed a pre-gig half pint of bitter before retiring to the dressing room with the other musicians.

'Where's Julie?' I first asked at around 7.30 and then at 7.45.

'It's still early,' said Eric.

'Why hasn't Nisha called round, or at least sent a message?'

'I'll call her on her mobile,' he replied.

'You've got a mobile? I thought that was only for City bankers.'

'Nah, lots of us have them these days. I think I've got her number programmed in. Here we go. Hello? Nisha? Where are you? Everything OK?' From the one side of the conversation, I could perceive that everything was clearly *not* OK. 'So, are you on your way…?' Interruption. 'Yes, but can you say when… Yes, Nish, yes, well I know she can be… So we'll see you….

OK, OK. Talk soon.' He hung up and looked up at me. 'All in hand,' he announced, nonchalantly.

'That is a transparent lie. It is obviously *not* all in hand,' I exploded. 'Why do you even say that?'

'Well it all will be in hand; just one or two things to iron out.'

'*Iron out*?' I shouted, but at that point my attention was distracted by someone tapping on my shoulder. I turned round to see the Reverend Godfrey Charlton, still in vicar's uniform, clearly not about to attend the party. 'What?!!' I said sharply, surprised, then softened my voice. 'Oh sorry, Godfrey, didn't mean to be rude. To what do we owe the pleasure?'

'I heard Jed Collins was playing.' He added with an apologetic air: 'I'm a bit of a fan.'

'From *whom* did you hear!?' I exploded. 'Who else knows? The whole town will bloody well turn up if we're not careful.'

'I didn't tell a soul,' he said. 'Mum's the word.' He pointed for no apparent reason to his nose.

What's the time? I asked myself. 8.10. Still no sign. 'Is it worth ringing Nisha again?' I asked Eric.

He wrinkled his nose and winced a little. 'I think that might be counter-productive.'

'What else can we do, then?'

'I'll get you another gin and tonic,' he replied.

'OK.'

Karen Harvey appeared. I had completely forgotten about her plea to be able to attend. As I was the only person she recognised, she came directly towards me. She was slightly out of breath. 'I'm not too late, am I? Traffic on the M23 was dreadful. Have I missed him?'

'No; you're in good time. Nice to see you. How's business?'

'Oh, fine. The City of London never sleeps.'

We began chatting about legal matters and were in mid-conversation when Elizabeth arrived and walked tentatively towards us. I caught her eye and thought I noticed, just for a nano second, a quiver of jealousy as she witnessed my amiable chat with an attractive woman of my age.

'Karen,' I said. 'I must interrupt you. I'd like to introduce you. Elizabeth, this is my fellow lawyer Karen Harvey, who helped set up this evening's events: Karen, may I introduce Elizabeth, my … my girlfriend.' I phrased the word with a little dramatic flourish. Smiles all round.

Then I remembered my responsibilities, and glanced down at my watch once more; nearly 8.30! I was about to sound the alarm, but at that moment Nisha finally burst through the door, with her mother and Julie following. Nisha caught sight of me, and, with the manner of a headmistress who has just discovered the culprit, marched smartly in my direction, while her Mum and Julie stayed talking quietly with each other. She then stood, hands on hips, looking at me with an expression of fierce determination, and made her speech with full stops peppered frequently through each sentence, by way of emphasis. She did not actually jab me in the chest with her forefinger to punctuate each phrase, but I sensed that such restraint had cost her effort: 'You. Have. Absolutely. No – 'scuse language – Fucking idea. How many lies. I have told. To get Julie Gray's butt down here tonight.'

'And a good evening to you too, Nisha. Nice to see your mother here.'

'She's only here because Jed Collins is singing – assuming you have got the real one to show up.'

'You told your *mother*??!! You're not supposed to tell anyone!' I said in an urgent stage whisper. 'The whole town and half of India are going to know by nine o'clock! It'll be on the news!'

'I had to! She kept chipping in on Julie's behalf – saying: "Oh, she can have a quiet night in for her birthday if she likes," "Stop pestering her, Nisha" "Julie's had a tough year", and all that. So I had to take her to one side and explain. Anyway, she agreed to persuade Julie, without letting on the full secret, but she wanted to come along as well. New problem: she had been going to be the babysitter for Jack and Hannah in the event of us going out. Fortunately, one of my sisters doesn't like Jed Collins and was free. So Mum ordered her to do the babysitting instead.'

'So, your Mum's a Jed Collins fan?'

'Everyone is, these days – well, except for my weird sister. The one who does art installations. He was in a Bollywood movie last year. Keep up. But the main thing is – Brian, Colin Clarke, whatever your name is. You owe me a favour. A big favour. I *will* call it in.'

'OK. Do you want to meet Jed Collins in the Green Room and have a glass of champagne with him?'

Her expression was transformed in an instant. She tucked her beautiful straight long black hair behind her right ear, beamed, and asked me: 'The real one?'

'Yes, the real one.'

Like a magician, from no discernable pocket or bag, she produced a stick of lipstick and touched up her lips; all movements apparently guided by instinct rather than conscious choice. 'Well, I guess that would qualify as favour returned. But I have had a stressful evening, so a *large* glass of champagne, and I will drink it slowly.' She added, after a pause: 'You've got a Green Room?'

'Well, we set one up, with the help of the hotel staff. There are a couple of sofas, a fridge and a buffet. He's brought some friends along – no, not his partner – so it's a bit of a party.'

'So, he's single – well for tonight?' she chuckled. She was not being serious, obviously.

'Don't get your hopes up,' I replied.

I guided her around the back of the hotel; we talked our way through the security folk. Jed Collins himself turned out to be a perfectly charming and pleasant young man, who actually looked you in the eye, rather than slightly above you in the manner of some famous folk. Nisha, to her credit, did not go all gooey, and held a perfectly relaxed conversation over her very large glass of bubbly from which she scarcely seemed to sip, keen to keep the moment going. I returned to the bar, largely to check that Julie hadn't fled.

'Julie,' I said to her. 'I'm very glad you made it here this evening. I know it's none of my business, but I want you to know that Eric is making huge efforts. He misses you.'

'I know,' she said. 'And thanks for all your help with him Brian, but it's not easy.' She looked desperately sad.

'OK.'

'Where's Nisha?' she asked. 'I was told there was going to be a gang of us girls here. I'm not staying around if it's speeches about cricket.'

'I promise – there will be none. And you won't be disappointed. No speeches; just a singer. Nisha's sorting out something very important.'

'She was very keen for me to come along, I'll say that,' commented Julie. 'It had better be worth it.'

After around 15 minutes of strained conversation with Julie – Eric tactfully stayed away, for now, I returned to fetch Nisha. 'Favour returned?'

'Favour returned,' she said.

'Good. Now come help me keep Julie at the venue.'

'Cool. I'll buy her her favourite cocktail.'

After a few instrumental numbers, which everyone treated largely as background music, Graham from behind his piano tapped loudly on a microphone and announced: 'And now we have a special guest vocalist…Maybe you can recognize who it's going to be from our introduction. First, however, can we ask one Julie Gray up on to the stage? Our guest singer wants to dedicate his first song especially to you.'

The band started up. Julie, after some hesitation, tiptoed up towards the stage area, looking terrified. One of the singer's assistants fetched her a chair. Some murmurs of anticipation passed around the hall as a recognisable song introduction began to become perceptible; a shared whisper of: 'Could it be *him*?'

The famous voice began a little before the man himself entered. Julie's eyes widened; still terrified but now entranced and shocked as well. He interrupted his own song introduction to say a few words: 'This song's for Julie Gray. It's a special request from her husband Eric for someone he describes as his beautiful but long-suffering wife.'

And he began. There were almost impossibly high-pitched squeals of delight from around the hall. Jed Collins made many swoon. Even I, a middle-aged heterosexual man, was mildly affected. Those green eyes; and a voice of perfect timbre.

Julie descended from the stage after the first number, keen to be away from the spotlight but clearly pleased at the gesture. She avoided looking at Eric. I looked across and he seemed nervous, before moving to an area well away from the stage, near the bar, to talk with Craig and a couple of other male friends I didn't recognise. Rather to my surprise, Julie took up residence next to me, with Nisha and mother to the left of her. Elizabeth was next to me, and Karen Harvey next to her; they had chatted and bonded a little. We stood near the edge of the dance-floor. After one song, Julie whispered to me: 'I have a feeling this is more your doing than Eric's, but thanks all the same.'

The singer's signature tune, *My Guardian Angel*, was saved 'til last. The lyrics were rather corny but the tune held together well and he sang it sweetly:

My guardian angel over me
My guardian angel by my side
When I was low
So very low
You came down and rescued me

'Hmm,' said Julie, swaying side to side in time with the gentle rhythm, humming the tune to herself, transfixed with rapture. 'Makes you wonder about the story behind it, doesn't it?'

'Indeed,' I replied. I looked over at Eric who, having grown a little bored of this girly music, was regaling Craig and his other mates, generating much laughter, with some tall sporty tale or filthy joke.

The concert passed off smoothly. There were no invasions of screaming teenage fans, or other security scares. At the end, Jed gave Julie a kiss on the cheek and a signed CD, and they posed for the arranged photograph. The tabloid newspaper had its exclusive news story. The PR lady Amy fussed about, never quite satisfied about anything.

As Julie retired once again from the stage and Jed was whisked away by his people, Eric finally found the courage to approach her. Unfortunately, perhaps, he was a little too direct: 'So are we back together?' he asked.

'Oh Eric it's not as easy as that,' she replied. 'But thank you so much for this. Thank you. And well done for getting sober and shaping up and going back to school. You're a real man. And a great Dad. Jack's proud of you, you know.'

She pecked him on the cheek, with affection but no more romantic desire than the singer had shown to her. Eric looked relieved and sad, in equal measure. They parted and joined their respective friends.

Elizabeth sidled up to me and placed her fingers through mine. She could see me looking wistfully towards them. 'You did warn me,' I observed. 'That things like this rarely go to plan.'

'Well, maybe it has gone to plan.'

'Hmm?'

'If they do separate, at least they won't hate one another. That's what matters most for the children and for them.'

'I guess so,' I replied, but I could not hide my disappointment that the evening did not end in Julie being swept up in his arms.

Graham wheeled himself over. 'Musicians are putting their kit away, can you help with the furniture and the PA?'

'Sure,' I replied. I turned to Elizabeth: 'See you later.'

With the singing star gone, the stage lights turned off and the hall lights lit, the excitement fell away and the atmosphere gained an air of anti-climax. Several people sauntered towards the exit, some chatting animatedly, others stayed in the hall. Godfrey, I noticed, left as soon as Jed had finished singing. The bar was still open. I stepped up on to the stage. Eric stepped up and joined me, glad for something practical to do. I looked around, but couldn't see Julie.

'Thanks for the help,' I said.

Graham called out: 'Can you begin turning the mics off? We're getting a bit of feedback and echo.'

'Will do!' I replied briskly, and began turning each off with a firm 'click', before continuing to chat with Eric.

'Will you have a meeting with Julie soon?' I inquired, hopefully.

'Mmm – ah, dunno,' he replied. 'There's too much stuff to say on both sides, I guess. Think I've blown it anyway. Way she looks at me now – she don't even see me any more.' Clearly keen not to discuss the matter further, he asked me: 'Good to see you with Elizabeth, then.'

'Yup – thanks for your advice.'

'What's your next step?'

'What? Are there "steps"? I don't know. I really don't know. The truth is, I love her. I love the bones of her. I love the very ground that she walks upon. I want to marry her, but I couldn't possibly ask. Obviously, if I thought she'd say yes, I'd ask her to marry me. But let's not rush her. It's too soon and – well, she might say no. That'd be one too many rejections for me, I think. It'd finish me off. Right, can you disconnect these microphones for me and put them away, now they're all turned off.'

'Um, I'm not entirely sure they are, Col.'

'What?' I looked up, and met his gaze for a few seconds. 'They are!' I insisted 'I turned them all off, one by one. No one's been up on the stage since.' Then I turned around at the hall and met 60 or 70 more gazes, Elizabeth's among them; all looking intently towards me. There was not a doubt that they had heard every word of our little chat; probably half the bar staff and the couple of taxi drivers just outside the main door had heard it too.

Eric rescued the situation, at least as best he could. He went up to the main microphone, still fixed in its stand just a foot or so away from me, inspected it and declared: 'Yes, this one is still "on", so I'd just like to say a few words on behalf of my mate Col, who was the brains behind the concert this evening. You thought you'd already seen the top of the bill this evening, but it turns out you hadn't, given his accidental little speech there. But I'd just like to point out that he's helped me this year you don't know how much. Don't think I'd have got through things without him. Elizabeth: it sounds like you and he need to take your conversation off somewhere private but, whatever you decide, bear in mind that he's the best bloke I've ever known.'

He earned an enthusiastic round of applause. I descended from the stage, red-faced, towards Elizabeth, who looked wryly amused at it all, and not the least embarrassed at being the focus of so much attention.

'Come on then, where is it?' She stretched out her left hand, fingers spread. She wore an amused grin.

'Where's what?'

'The ring, silly.'

'What? Is that a yes?'

'Well, if you can propose by accident, I may choose to accept.'

'I turned the microphone off, honest!' I protested. 'I'm so sorry.'

'Well, someone must have turned it back on.'

'No one walked by!'

'Maybe it was an angel.'

'We have an angel?'

'That's where the evidence is pointing.'

'Well, I hadn't actually planned this; I don't have a ring. Even if I had planned it all, I wouldn't have expected you to say yes. I'll go to Bond Street – first thing in the morning.'

'Fine! I'll be waiting. On the train platform; that's romantic.'

'I note that, even in this age of equality, it's still the man who has to take the initiative, organize things, and pick up the bill.'

'Well, you like to keep some traditions going,' she replied cheekily. 'I'm kind of doing you a favour, really.'

'It's very generous of you.'

'So, my fiancé,' she said to me in a saucy voice, clasping her hand in mine. 'There's no reason that we can't have a romantic ending. Shall we go back to your place?'

'Elizabeth! We're not married yet!'

'Well, we're no spring chickens either. Sex is even more exciting when it's forbidden. I read about that in a book this summer.'

'Yes, well, you don't have to read a book to work that one out.'

Epilogue

Just a couple of weeks after my accidental proposal, Godfrey pulled me to one side just before the service, as I was about to enter church.

'Colin,' he said, with some urgency, as he took me by the arm and manoeuvred me to one side, near the entrance porch. 'I have tell you something! I've been asked to read the banns for Elizabeth Giles, spinster of the neighbouring parish, and she's marrying this chap called Brian Clarke. I don't know if you knew. He's from this parish, as it happens. I'm so sorry – I really thought you and she were perfect for each other, which is why I introduced her to you. I knew you were fond of her and I thought you ought to know.'

'That's really OK Godfrey, in fact....'

'Well, you're taking it very well. And they're rushing too; I've been asked for some dates in the new year for the ceremony itself. I have to dash, sorry – perhaps I'll see you soon, well not at the wedding obviously, but at a service before long?'

'Actually, Godfrey, I will be at the wedding.'

'Really? That's very Christian of you.'

'I would want Elizabeth to be happy. In fact, I'll make a point of not only attending – but making sure I get there in good time.'

'Well, that is very generously spirited of you, Colin,' said Godfrey, a look of surprise still frozen on his face.

Sadly, I was unable to keep the secret until the big day itself – his face would have been a picture – as there were preparations to take part in. To this day, however, he often gives me an odd look as he struggles to be certain of how to address me.

The wedding itself passed by with only one major hitch. As Godfrey asked if there was anyone who knew of any just cause or impediment, there was a sharp cry of 'Yes!' from the back of the church. The two of us looked at each other in horror, Elizabeth doubtless wondering how she had missed my secret first wife in her visit to the attic, fearful of an attorney's march down the aisle. It transpired that the cry had come from Tony, listening to the football radio commentary via an earpiece, who became over-excited as Brighton & Hove Albion unexpectedly took the lead away to a top division side in an FA Cup tie. His mother marched him out by the ear, like a five year old. The service proceeded. With inspired improvisation, Godfrey announced: 'I now pronounce you man and wife,' – after pausing for the round of applause he added: 'But next, the half-time scores.'

Nearly twenty years have passed. Elizabeth and I are now white-haired, and even more fond of reading and the countryside than before. We still go to church, of course, in part for the company and the readings, having concluded that whether or not God exists is more for him to worry about, than for us. We had hoped, with Elizabeth being under 45, that a baby was possible, but she (or he – I'm getting used to the vernacular of equality) did not come along. There are many consolations, including our step-grandchildren: Shelley and Dale got married and had two boys and two girls – all lively and charming. The eight of us had a holiday in a caravan park on the south coast and I have never witnessed such irrepressible joy as exhibited by their children on the beach, in the playground and in the ten-pin bowling hall (where I beat Dale twice consecutively, by the way).

We never did move house. The old one just needed sprucing up. The floorings were too dark and old; the wallpaper had to go. The dusty curtains were replaced with bright, modern shutters. The kitchen had been all wrong, apparently. So that got sorted out.

I still play, occasionally, opening the batting for the third team, having overcome my playing-field snobbishness, and turning out on the recreation grounds and village fields, even scoring the occasional half-century. I did finally relent and buy a protective helmet for batting. Last April, retrieving my cricket gear from the top shelf of the conservatory, ready for the new season, it fell off and the edge of the visor caught me just above the eye. Needed three stitches. So that was ironic.

The young lads in the first team are very focused and fit, these days. There are no more beer jugs, though they do at least have nicknames. The Fines Master as an institution has been phased out – well, except for the tour, obviously. When someone drops a catch in a league match these days they are given encouraging noises, not a volley of insults and a 30p fine. Some of the younger players have been known to go to the gym and watch their diet. Still, none has yet beaten the club record aggregate for a season that I set in 1989 of 1,617 runs (average 64.68, three centuries). I had to look those stats up of course – it's not like I've memorized them or anything.

Eric and Julie never did get back together, but each found a loving new partner. It helps that Julie is not with the man of the bedroom incident, but someone else, and by all accounts a decent individual and a responsible step-dad. Eric met a lovely young woman at his evening classes. She already had a son from a scoundrel of an ex-boyfriend. They had two more together. Both families (or is it just one extended family?) meet up for barbeques sometimes. It's not what the Bible envisaged, but you cannot deny the human love.

Jack now plays for Brighton & Hove Albion, first team, with a proud Dad watching every home game; sometimes he has invited me along. Eric shouts at the referee every time that young Jack is obstructed, pushed or has his shirt pulled, which is pretty much every time he gets the ball – well, in Eric's view, anyway. Better, Eric insisted that the young lad sat his A-Levels, and treats his girlfriend well.

Jack's first team captain was one Benjamin Hilaire, some ten years his senior – so I get to meet proud Dad Jeffrey again, and his lovely wife Janine, which was very emotional when we were reunited! They are now quite grey and grandparents. Jeffrey got promoted to become a senior manager at a local authority. The only bowling he does now is underarm to the grandchildren 'My back went when I was 50', but I bet he troubles them in the 'corridor' outside off stump. Janine is also a social worker and a bookworm. She and Elizabeth bonded immediately over Charlotte Bronte and Andrea Levy (not Jane Austen – too twee, apparently). They talk about the lack of an arc in post-modern literature, while Jeffrey and I discuss how to spot a googly and the slope at Lord's. The only thing that makes us sad is the unexpected decline in West Indies cricket.

Benjamin finished his degree at Birmingham University, and plans to set up a business when he's too old to play football professionally. So that family is in very good shape. Benjamin and Jack sometimes co-host events for the charity Kick Racism out of Football. They are an absolute credit to their dads. Sometimes, I think that young men today are rather better behaved than we Baby Boomers: they help about the house more, they drink less, they're less likely to be racially prejudiced.

Iain and Jed had their civil partnership in the first month possible, December 2005. They now live on a Mediterranean island, which they probably own, have adopted five children and run a sanctuary for threatened species. Iain set up and lavishly funds a charity for vulnerable and suicidal teenagers, called 'Guardian Angels'.

Elizabeth still engages far more in good works than hedonism, but has unfortunately taken more of a liking for even edgier rock music as she gets older, and plays Led Zeppelin and the like. She is particularly fond of this track called 'All Right Now' by a group called Free, and dances around the living room to it. I protest that it's garish and modern and she replies nonsense – it's more than 40 years old. Of course, it's perfectly possible that she plays it primarily to encourage me out of my armchair to do some gardening. I am worried she'll experiment with cocaine before long. But apart from that, everything's fine. I think I've managed to become a genial old soul, and not a curmudgeonly old git. But it was touch and go at times.

Suggested questions for Book Clubs

1. Brian is in his 40s, has never married, and lives in the house he spent most of his childhood. Do you think his caution is innate, or more a product of circumstance?

2. What do you think Elizabeth finds attractive about him given that, outwardly, she would appear to have more in common with her left-wing hiking friends?

3. Elizabeth is unhappy about sections of the Bible, and left the convent because of an unrequited love. Do you think there are other factors in her doubts, and worries about her faith?

4. How significant is Brian's long-term friendship with Jeffrey, given that they only meet once or twice a year?

5. Elizabeth rebukes Brian for his apparent double standards on casual sex. Do you think she is too harsh?

6. Do you think Elizabeth regrets the extent to which she devoted the early years of her adult life to others? Does she feel guilt over that regret?

7. Why do you think Brian cried for the first time in his life, while on holiday in Toledo, reading about the slave trade?

8. Why do you think his thoughts during such a short holiday had such a profound impact on his world view?

9. Julie seems to put up with Eric's laddish, drunken behaviour for quite a few years. What do you think was going on there?

10. What impact did the behaviour of Eric's father have on his life?

11. Discuss the friendship between Brian and Eric, and the differences in their social background.

12. And finally .... Does anyone believe in Guardian Angels?

Author photo copyright 'Natalia Creative'

PJ Whiteley, who writes non-fiction as Philip Whiteley, is an experienced author, principally in the field of management. He has written extensively about how low wages are bad for business, as part of a bid to try to convince economists that society consists of people. Taking a break from this Quixotic task, he has turned his hand to romantic comedy, seizing on the potential of men preferring to play or watch sport than talk about their feelings and stuff.

Close of Play is his first novel, centring on perennial themes of the human condition: love, loss, hope, life choices and that nagging feeling in the back of the mind that you may not fully be up to date with how your team is doing.

PJ Whiteley's boyhood ambition was to represent Yorkshire Cricket Club. He gave up playing as an amateur a few years ago when facing the quicker bowlers became a bit too tricky, but still plays five-a-side football. He works from home full time as an author and is married to a sex therapist, so things could have turned out worse.